RAGE

UNTAMED SONS MC MANCHESTER CHAPTER

PART ONE

JESSICA AMES

MANCHESTER CHAPTER
RAGE
UNTAMED SONS MC BOOK SIX

USA TODAY BESTSELLING AUTHOR
JESSICA AMES

Copyright © 2023 by Jessica Ames

www.jessicaamesauthor.com

Rage is a work of fiction. Names, places, characters, and incidents are a product of the author's imagination and are fictitious. Any resemblance to actual persons living or dead, events, or establishments is solely coincidental.

Editing - Dark Syde Edits

Proofreader – Gem's Precise Proofreads

Alpha Readers – Jayne Ruston, Clara Martinez Turco, Jenni Oldham

Beta Readers – Lynne Garlick, Lisa Foot, Karen Kerr, Kara Paquin Merideth, Marie Jackson

Please note: this book contains material aimed at an adult audience, including sex, violence, and bad language.

All rights reserved. Except as permitted under Copyright Act 1911 and the Copyright Act 1988, no part of this publication may be reproduced, distributed, or transmitted in any form or by any means, or stored in a database or retrieval system, without the prior express written consent of the author.

This book is covered under the United Kingdom's Copyright Laws. For more information visit: www.gov.uk/copyright/overview

AUTHOR'S NOTE

This book contains upsetting themes. For a full list of these themes visit:
https://www.jessicaamesauthor.com/jessicaamestwcw

This book is set in the United Kingdom. Some spellings may differ.

CHAPTER 1
RAGE

P*ast...*

There isn't much that scares me, but the darkness of the room has the fine hairs on my arms standing up. Usually, I can see out of the small window that overlooks the high-rise behind our building, but there is a sheet of plywood covering the frame, blocking out any hint of light that might chase the shadows away.

That's new.

He's never done that before. Has my father's tenuous grip on reality finally slipped beyond any doctor's ability to fix?

Trying to peer through the inky blackness suffocating me, I take slow, steady breaths. My heart is racing, and the back of my neck feels clammy, but I force myself to remain unfazed. This room means something bad is coming. It means he's having one of *those* days.

Cold spreads through every molecule of my body. Aged injuries flare, remembering old pains. There is a spot on my back, just around my kidneys, that still aches even though it has been healing for months.

I close my eyes, though there is no need. I'm already surrounded by darkness, but this feels like shutting the world out completely. I need to do that, not because I'm scared, but for a different reason. The fear that used to nip at my heels when he put me in this room has been replaced by something else, something far more sinister.

Anger.

I feel the rage bubbling inside me, a dormant volcano biding its time before it erupts. My body sings with the need to release it, but I'm terrified if I do, I'll never be able to shut it off.

For months, it has been growing, getting stronger and more potent. Every wound he has inflicted on me is another mark against him, another link in the chain I plan to beat him with. The injustice of my suffering burns through me like fire. I've been on a back foot for too long. He has kept me cowed and afraid, but no more.

I won't let him hurt me, not this time. I'm no longer that little kid he can push around. I've grown inches in the past month, and I stand taller than him for the first time in my life. If he wants to fight me, I'll give as good as I get.

It won't fix the past, but it might redeem my present. There are scars I can't heal, too many littering my body, but I'm done being a helpless bystander in my own life. I want him to suffer the way I have. I want him to feel the pain of rejection and disgust.

I don't know how long I've been locked in this room—time has no meaning when it is constantly dark—but it has given my brain the opportunity to work overtime. Hate and fury has spread through me like a poison until it's all I can think of. I want him dead. I want to destroy him in the way he has me.

My father has never cared a single day for my happiness. Not when I was born, and not when that bitch dropped me off on his doorstep either. Dear old Mum took care of me for the first three years of my life before she decided she'd done enough parenting and the sperm donor needed to take his turn raising the kid neither of them wanted.

That was the start of my nightmare.

I have known pain at the hands of my father every moment since she dumped me on him. It was never as bad as this, not in the beginning, but for the past two years, it has felt as if he's lost control. He wants to destroy me, to punish me for what he sees as me ruining his life.

Maybe I have.

I'm not the easiest kid. I'm always in trouble at school, at least when he allows me to leave the flat to go. There should be lines of social workers and teachers questioning my absence, but I'm a problem, and these people don't want me out there causing more trouble. Better to let me slip away as if I never existed.

Then I'm no one's issue.

I'm only fourteen years old and already written off by

the systems put in place to protect kids like me. That hurts more than it should. It breaks through the thick walls I've erected around my heart.

No one cares. Not my mum, not my father, not my teachers, not society either. No one will save me from this horror. I'm on my own.

That should be a lonely feeling. Instead, it fans the flames burning in my gut higher. I'm done being a victim.

I draw my knees to my chest, wrapping my arms around them as my teeth grind together. I'm not patient, and I'm eager to get this over with, but I've been locked in here for so long, or at least that is how it feels. My father won't come to me until he is good and ready.

So, I count.

I count all the ways I'm going to hurt him.

I count them over and over, repeating all the things I'm going to do to him.

Burn him.

Cut him.

Hit him.

Hurt him.

I've done this for months, but I've never had the guts to follow through with any of my plans. Today, I may not have the strength to do what I want either, but I'm more determined than ever to make him pay.

It makes me feel better to imagine his death, his torment and torture at my hands, even if I can't go through with it.

Movement beyond the door has my head snapping in that direction. A slither of light suddenly appears at the base of the frame. He's removing the tape, piece by piece. I'm not sure when he came up with the idea of putting duct tape around the frame, but it covers every crack, making sure I can see nothing of the world outside this room.

Scrambling to my feet, I watch as more light appears inch by inch. Accustomed to the darkness of the room, the light has the shadowy shapes of the furniture in the room take form.

I curl my fingers into fists at my side, my lips pulling into a snarl.

Today is the day.

I'm going to make him hurt.

Waiting for the tape to be removed seems to take an eternity, but eventually, I hear the key scrape in the lock before it twists.

I wince against the flood of light as the door opens, raising my hand to cover my face. It burns my eyes, creating prisms of colour in my vision that I blink away quickly.

The monster who has made my life a misery is silhouetted in the frame. My mouth dries, but I try to hold onto the anger and push aside my fear. I won't hide or run. Not this time.

He doesn't seem to notice the internal struggle I'm having as he crosses the space, grabbing me around the throat. As soon as he touches me, I forget about my promise to destroy him. Terror wraps around my heart, strangling its ability to pump as my back hits the wall behind me.

I'm weak, pathetic—all the things he tells me I am. If I was strong, I would fight him. I would shove him back and defend myself. Instead, I do nothing other than try to breathe through my growing panic.

He pins me with his eyes, which even in the shitty lighting, I can tell are filled with resentment.

You're nothing.
You're pathetic.
You'll never be anything.

My father has never had a problem with telling me how much of a disappointment I am.

His eyes scan mine, darting back and forth maniacally. My heart thuds as I brace for what is coming next.

"The devil is in you, boy," he whispers.

Looking into his eyes is like peering into a mirror. We both have the same features, right down to the slope of our noses. I don't remember what features, if any, I got from the bitch who birthed me.

Am I as screwed up as him?
Is this going to be my future?
Will I lose my mind, just as he has?
Will I hurt and destroy the people around me just as my father has?

I don't know what he did to my mother, but she dumped me with him and never once came back. What kind of mother does that?

One who is scared for her life.

I hate myself for justifying her behaviour, but I can't help it. I want desperately to believe my mother was as much a victim of the beast she left me with as I am, because the alternative is she left me here knowing what he would do to me.

I can't understand how she could do that to her own child.

How can my father do the things he does to me?

"I'm good," I promise him, my voice wobbling. "I don't have evil in me. You purged it last time, remember?"

Mentally, I urge him to recall the last torture session he inflicted on me, and for it to be enough to stop this madness.

I watch his mind working, trying to understand what I'm saying. His fingers don't leave my throat as his eyes narrow on me.

"You're trying to trick me."

"I'm not."

"The devil plays games." He shakes his head as if trying to clear it. "I have to purge the evil from you."

It's those words that enables me to ruthlessly shove my terror aside. I won't do another 'purging'. I won't let him cleanse me. The last time I thought I was going to die. It didn't seem possible to feel so much pain and still be breathing.

I cling to the anger that scorches through me. My innocence has been stripped away piece by piece, along with my joy and my ability to love and to feel.

He has destroyed everything I am and is responsible for the darkness he has sown inside me. I didn't have the devil inside me before him.

I grit my teeth, glaring at my father as my rage mounts inside me. My fear is dissipating like steam.

"Fuck… *you*." I spit the words out through tight lips.

Dad tightens his grip on my throat. I have to fight, have to hold on to the rage inside me. If I don't, I'm going to die in this room. I still might.

"That's the devil talking," he hisses at me.

I close my eyes as he takes me down onto my back in a move so violent, it slams my teeth together. The floor beneath me is hard, and my spine aches. His fingers grapple to lift my T-shirt, exposing my stomach.

I can't do this.

Not again.

I hear the click of the lighter and smell the burning tobacco as it infuses the air. I brace, ready for what is about to happen. I hate this. I hate him.

The pain as the lit end of the cigarette presses into the soft flesh of my stomach makes me swallow a scream. I can't make a sound. If I do, he'll come at me harder. The purging of evil from my body is meant to be serene. It's anything but.

I try to ignore the agony spreading through me as the ember burns through my skin, but I can't.

Red rage boils through my blood, pumping around my body with a blast of adrenaline. I grab his wrist, a mistake I've made before and been beaten worse for, but this time, I'm not letting it go that far. My father gasps as I squeeze him with every ounce of strength I have.

And that is a good amount.

I might be a kid, but I'm also tall for my age and I've grown into my body lately. I'm not that weak kid he can push around. I'm also determined. I'm fighting for my survival, and that gives me a boost of strength.

Opening my eyes, I meet his confused but furious gaze.

"The devil doesn't want to come out of you, Beau."

I blow air through my nose like a bull ready to charge. "That's where you're wrong. You're about to meet him in full force."

I shove him back, and the element of surprise means I'm able to unseat him from me. He falls back onto the floor as the cigarette rolls away. I don't chase it. I have better weapons at my disposal.

Clamouring to my feet, I stumble to my father and unleash everything I have. My father taught me violence, and I repay those lessons without any remorse.

My foot slams into his side over and over. He tries to stand, to escape my unrelenting attack, but I don't give him a second of reprieve. My blood pumps furiously through my veins, and my pulse hammers in my throat as I beat the man who is supposed to love me.

All my years of suffering, of being afraid, are released from behind the dam I've kept up. I kick him so hard, my foot aches, my legs too, but I don't stop, roaring into the air as I go on.

He cowers, blood pouring down his face. The man I feared, the man who instilled terror in me is in this moment reduced to a shell. It gives me even more strength to fight him. He's not scary. He's a fucking coward.

"You will never touch me again." I spit the words savagely.

The smell of something burning fills my nose, and the flicking orange light catches my attention. The fire is small, crackling as it takes hold. The acrid scent of the carpet melting fills my nose and tickles my throat. I cough, pressing my face against the crook of my elbow as I try to find clean air to breathe in.

My father crawls back from the heat, his eyes frantic. "The flames of hell have come for us!"

"They're here for you, you piece of shit," I hiss at him.

His mind is broken, and for a split second, I feel regret —not for him, but for me. I never had the parents I wanted, the life I needed. Those fuckers couldn't even get the basic things right. I grit my teeth until my jaw aches.

"Burn in hell." I glare down at him, and then I turn and leave the room, ignoring his whimpers behind me.

I feel detached, like I'm moving on autopilot as I head for the front door. I grab his keys from the bowl near the front door, and then I unlock it and step out onto the walkway. The air is clean and my lungs ache from breathing in the smoke for even a moment. The door is PVC, solid, with no way to unlock it without the key.

It's cold, but I put the key in and twist it, locking my father inside the burning flat. There's no way out. The windows on the back are high off the ground. The one on the front is too small for even a child to get through.

I step back from the door, my heart thudding. The fire will be spreading, and he'll be breathing in the toxic smoke. I should care, feel something, but I don't.

I glance up the walkway, expecting to see people witnessing the evil I'm carrying out, but there's no one. It's odd because this walkway is usually filled with residents hanging out of their flats, socialising, and drinking or smoking.

But there is no one, and that makes me feel justified.

The universe doesn't want this bastard saved.

I make my way to the stairs leading down to the ground level. When I reach the bottom, I wander across the parking area before glancing back up at the building. There's no smoke or flames, nothing to show the turmoil happening inside the flat right now.

I tighten my jaw as I toss the keys into a bush at the edge of the tarmac.

That fuck can burn in hell, and if there's any justice in this world, he will.

CHAPTER 2
SKYE

"Time to get up, Skye-bug."

I groan at Tommy's voice as it blasts too close to my ear before reaching for my pillow to pull it over my head. The grittiness of my eyes tells me it's too early to be awake, and the comfiness of my bed makes me want to sink back into sleep.

Tommy has other ideas. He grabs the pillow, dragging it away from my face, and a feral hiss escapes my mouth as I open my eyes to glare at him.

Dark hair flops into his eyes, which are sparkling with amusement. I narrow mine, squinting at him through my hazy vision. "Does my dad know you're in my bedroom?" I huff out my irritation, trying to snatch my duvet over myself.

"Desmond loves me," he says in a tone that makes me want to punch him.

"He's going to stop loving you when I tell him you invaded my bedroom and tried to drag me out of bed."

The grin that splits his face loosens some of the tension inside me. It's impossible to be pissed when he's standing in front of me looking like this.

"Who do you think sent me?"

I sit up so fast, my head spins. The covers fall back, revealing the tiny camisole top I'd slipped into before going to sleep last night. I don't try to hide my body, not from Tommy.

"Dad's here?" I move before he has a chance to answer, throwing my duvet back and scrambling out of the bed.

"I'm here too, bug," he grumbles without any real heat. He knows I love him. I have from the moment we were little babies. Tommy is my best friend and the person I've relied on my entire life. There's a reason my dad sent him to wake me up. I'm not a morning person, and anyone else would've got a mouthful of abuse from me.

"You're always here," I dismiss, rushing over to my walk-in closet and scanning the shelves for something to pull on that won't make my dad's head explode.

Tommy follows me, leaning against the door jamb, his arms folding over his chest. The skinny boy I grew up with has disappeared beneath a mass of muscle. He's broader and harder, even behind the smiles and jokes he gives me.

That's what my father's business does to the men who follow him. It takes their joy and their easement and creates soulless shells. Tommy isn't there yet, but I see the darkness creeping in a little every day.

The thought has me pausing as I fumble through a stack of leggings in the cubby in front of me. "Are you working for my dad full-time now?" I try to keep the question light, easy, but my words are choked as they slip between my lips.

I don't dare look at him, even as the silence grows. I wish I wasn't in this closet—the walls feels too close.

"It's what we do," he says finally. "My family has been part of the Pioneers for generations."

A knot tangles in my gut, and I grip the edge of the cubby, trying to ground the panic swirling through me. "What about university?"

We'd sat around the kitchen table only a month ago talking about our dreams and ambitions for the future. Even then, I knew it was a foolish girl's fantasy, but I hoped I could save my friend from the horrors that await him in my father's organisation.

"Ain't smart enough for uni." He scoffs, sounding unlike the boy I know.

Because he's not a boy.

Tommy is eighteen, and in our world, he's a man. With that comes responsibilities and demands. I take a second to mourn the loss of the life we had before we both became adults.

"You're plenty smart," I mumble, resuming my search for leggings.

Finding a pair, I turn around and grab a sweater from the pile on the shelf. I can't look at him. This isn't the life I wanted for Tommy. He's not like the others.

His hand circles my bicep as tears threaten to blossom in my eyes. The grip he has on me is solid but not designed to hurt. Tommy would never do anything to harm me.

"Bug, look at me."

I don't want to, but his insistence has me lifting my eyes to meet his. Dark brown orbs focus on me with laser precision. "You don't have to have this life, Tommy."

He laughs under his breath, a sharp sound that is missing his usual mirth. "I was born into this as much as you were. This is all we were ever going to be."

I refuse to believe that. My father's path is not mine, but had I been born with a cock, my lazy mornings and university applications I've been wading through all summer wouldn't be happening. He indulges me because I'm a girl and he doesn't know what else to do with me.

"No." The word is soft but filled with defiance. "You can be whoever you want to be."

There's that dark laugh again. I don't like it, not from him. "This is who I want to be," he says, as if he's forgotten all those talks we had about our aspirations.

"You don't. You never have."

It's the wrong thing to say. He snaps his spine straight, adding a few inches to his already out of control height. The way he looms makes him seem threatening, and if he were anyone else, I might be afraid.

"I'm a Pioneer. I was born into this life, and I ain't walking away. Jack says—"

The scowl that scrunches up my face at his name is uncontrollable. "Fuck Jack," I snap.

Tommy's shoulders tighten at my disrespect. I should

shut my mouth and stop talking, but I can't. My fear for Tommy outweighs everything else.

"Don't talk like that." There's a coldness in his tone that I've never heard from him, and it makes my skin prickle.

"You're not one of them." I don't know if I'm begging or telling him this, but my throat feels constricted as I force the words out.

Tommy's mouth pulls into a tight line, and his brows narrow together as he stares down at me. "Get dressed, Skye."

No 'Bug', no warmth either, and as I watch him walk away, I take the dismissal as if he's punched me in the stomach. I should stop him, but I stand still until I hear my bedroom door open and then snick shut.

My breath rips out of me as I try to calm the thudding of my heart. I don't want to fight with him, but Tommy isn't like my father's men. He doesn't have that same ruthless streak.

Does he?

The question slides through my thoughts without warning. I'm in denial and I know it. Over the past month, maybe, Tommy has started to change, though I don't want to admit it. I don't want to lose my friend, not to my father and his fucking organisation.

Numb to everything, I dress quickly and pull a brush through my hair before I slip the mask into place. I can't show my disappointment and fear without disrespecting Tommy. In private, it's okay to question him, but I know better than to do it in front of my dad.

I steel my spine and take a deep breath before I leave my bedroom. My childhood home is sprawling, and memories are embedded in every corner of it. A lot of those memories have Tommy front and centre.

As I take the stairs down to the ground floor, I spot one of my father's guards waiting by the front door. He acknowledges me with a slight movement of his head, even though he has known me since I was in nappies.

I am a jewel meant only to be looked at but never touched. I hate that most of all. I don't want or need to be treated like I'm special, but the men in my father's life treat me like a precious stone.

The kitchen is usually where my father gathers when he comes to the house. I figure that's because he knows he's not staying long enough to get comfortable. Dad isn't even a weekend parent—sometimes he's gone for weeks at a time, even months. I have minders, and up until two years ago, I had a nanny who took care of everything, including schooling.

Now, it's just me and a bunch of guards who are meant to die for me if my father's enemies find the house. I hate knowing that, but these men willingly put their lives on the line to be part of Desmond Richardson's empire.

Just like Tommy.

I ignore the taunting voice as I push open the door to the kitchen and step into the room.

My father is sitting at the kitchen table which overlooks the vast gardens and stables beyond. Tommy is leaning a hip against the breakfast bar, his eyes alert, but they don't come to me, which cuts deeper than it should.

Standing near the bifold doors that span the back of the room is Jack. He and Tommy could be twins. They both have the same dark hair and chocolate orbs that see too much, but warmth has been extinguished in Jack's completely. He is tethered to my dad in a way that scares me. The few years he has on Tommy have chipped away at any kindness he had before. Now, he wears that same look in his eyes as all the men my father leads. He's seen too much, done too much, and all that innocence he had has been stripped away.

I glance at Tommy, knowing that one day he'll become like his brother.

"Skye," he murmurs as I pass him.

"Hey, Jack." It's all I say because I know he won't offer more conversation. He never does.

Instead, I go to my father and wrap my arms around his neck, hugging him so tightly, I must be cutting off his air supply. He doesn't complain or try to pull me free. He holds me against him, his fingers pressing against my back in a way that makes me feel safe.

I struggle to reconcile the man holding me with the one who is taking my best friend from me. These mixed emotions make my head fuzzy. I love my father, and he loves me, but I hate the other side of him, the one that isn't my parent.

Desmond Richardson is a feared man. I've heard the stories about him, read them too, but to me, he's just my dad. I've rarely seen that dark side of him, and I never want to.

"That's the kind of welcome I could get used to," he says against my hair.

I don't want to let him go, but I'm aware we're not alone. The unspoken rules of our world are so ingrained in me that I pull back before I want to. Every time he leaves me, I know it could be the last. Over the years, my father has been in hospital with injuries more times than I can count from other gangs taking shots at him or trying to run him off the road. Once, two men broke into his suite in the city. He was stabbed six times and lost almost half his blood before he was found.

Those dark thoughts sit in my mind constantly when he's gone from the house. I learned early on to always savour those hugs because it could be the last one I ever give him.

Dad seems oblivious to my internal unrest as he gestures for me to sit opposite him at the table.

I do as he asks, pulling out the chair. I wish I could protect Tommy from him. It stirs my feelings in an uncomfortable way.

How can I love my father so completely when he is taking one of the most important people in my life from me?

My jaw aches from forcing a smile I don't feel, but I so rarely get to see my dad, and I don't want to say anything that might make him leave.

"Why are you here?" The question comes out more abrupt than I intend.

"A father can't visit his daughter to wish her a happy birthday?"

I don't point out that my birthday was two weeks ago. Perhaps I should've been disappointed when he didn't show up to give me presents and make my day special, but I know who he is and what he's capable of. I take every scrap of affection he gives me because I know it costs him dearly to do it.

"Of course, you can." I smile, and it's genuine. I am glad to see him, even if he looks tired and worn. "Are you sleeping?" The question slips out before I can stop it.

Dad laughs but turns to Tommy and Jack. "Give us the room."

Both leave without question, though Tommy glances back at me before he steps through the door. I used to be able to read his every nuance, but I don't know what he's trying to convey with that look. Further proof that I am losing him to my dad.

"I brought you something," he says when we're alone.

Excitement floods my veins as he pulls out a small package. It's gift-wrapped in pretty paper with ribbons. "You pay extra to have it wrapped?" I ask, smiling.

He snorts. "In eighteen years, have you ever seen me wrap a fucking present?"

I haven't and the thought is ludicrous.

I take the gift and unwrap it, struggling to get the paper off in one stubborn spot where the shop assistant has used too much cellotape. Eventually, I reveal a dark blue box with the name of a jeweller I love.

There is a part of me that knows this is my father's way of keeping my love, but this is how it has always been between us.

Carefully, I prise the box open, a flash of silver shimmering as I get a look at the beautiful bracelet inside. There is a heart charm attached to it, encrusted in diamonds and rubies. It's subtle yet clearly expensive. I take it out the box and hand it to my father to place on my wrist, which he does.

"I love it, thank you." I twist my arm to look at it in place.

"The sales girl picked it out," he admits.

He can't possibly let me believe that he chose it himself. I shake my head, laughing a little. If only his enemies knew he was picking out gifts for his daughter.

"I love it no matter what," I amend. I fiddle with the delicate precious metal against my skin, trying to work up the courage to broach Tommy with my dad. "I haven't seen you in a while." I settle on this topic instead. It's not even close to what I want to say, but I've learnt warming my father up is helpful in these kinds of situations.

"Been busy."

It's a sidestep, but I expect that.

"I worry about you." That's not a lie. I worry about him every moment of every day. Each call that comes in I fret could be to tell me his dangerous life has finally caught up with him.

"I'm fine."

I don't push it, even though I want to. The older I get, the harder it is to accept the lies he tells me. "Tommy's spending more time with you," I say.

He picks up the mug in front of him and takes a sip of the coffee in it. There's no rush to answer me. As always,

Desmond Richardson is in control, even if it's just of the conversation.

"Dad?" I press when he doesn't speak.

"He was always destined to be one of my boys," he says finally, placing his mug back on the tabletop.

I want to beg him to release Tommy from this unspoken contract, but I know he will never allow it, and Tommy would kill me for even asking.

"He's not like Jack," I say.

I hate having to deliver that truth about Tommy, but I would never forgive myself if I say nothing and he gets killed serving my father.

"No, he's better than Jack."

I frown. "How?"

"This shit isn't your business, kid." He emphasises the last word, telling me that despite the fact I'm recently eighteen, I am still a child in his eyes. "But I know you aren't going to let this go, so I'm going to lay it out for you. Tommy's family belongs to the Pioneers. Those boys were born to it. Jack is an asset, but Tommy? He has more potential than his brother ever will have. He cares and he loves deeply. When you got something to fight for, you fight harder."

Bile coats the back of my throat. He plans to use that softness in Tommy as a weapon?

"Please, Daddy, let him go."

"Wish I could, darlin', but I can't. Tommy deserves his chance."

"But—"

"Enough." He doesn't shout the word; he doesn't have

to. That crack of authority in his voice is enough to silence me. Nothing I say will change his mind, and trying to push it will just make him more annoyed, which could blow back on Tommy.

I don't want that, so I hold my tongue.

"Are you staying long?" I change the subject—an olive branch.

He takes it. "I just came to drop off your present."

That's a stab to the heart, but I take it without making a sound. I should be used to this by now, but it hurts just as much as it did when I was younger.

"Okay," I tell him, even though it's not. It'll never be.

Dad's gaze shifts to the bifold doors overlooking the gardens. "I didn't just come here to give you the gift."

My body stiffens at the seriousness of his tone. "You didn't?"

"I learnt something that's troubling me."

Cold spreads through me at the clipped tone of his voice. "What?"

He sniffs, a tic he's always had when he's stressed, which heightens my own anxiety.

"I love you, Skye. I know I don't always show it how you want, and fuck, if your mum was still here, she'd do enough loving for us both." It's rare for my dad to open up like this, so I don't speak, letting him get the words out that he needs to. "You're eighteen now. An adult. If you were a man, I'd already have you in my ranks, watching my back."

I wonder where this is going. "You changed your mind about recruiting me?" It's said in jest but also to test the water. I know my father believes I could never be an asset to his organisation.

"I think you know what I'm talking about."

"I don't," I disagree.

"I know about your applications to universities outside the city."

Fuck. I'd hoped to keep that a secret for a while longer. My mind whirls. How did he find out?

"I don't want to let you go, sweetheart, but I also know I can't keep you locked up either. I'll indulge your plans to study, but whatever thoughts you have of moving away, put them out of your head. You ain't going. There are plenty of good universities in the city, so pick the one you want and I'll arrange everything."

The only person I told that I was applying for schools farther afield was Scarlett, and I know she would never spill my secrets. She and I share a bond that no one outside our world can understand. Like me, Scarlett was born into this world. Her dad is a Pioneer, and her uncle and her brothers too.

Growing up, we went to the same parties and events, which unsurprisingly cemented our friendship. We bonded over our shared trauma of having criminals for fathers.

I know she wouldn't spill my secrets, which means Dad found out another way. Considering he monitors every aspect of my life, it's not a leap to assume he's aware of what I've been up to.

"The course I'm looking at is only available at certain universities. None of which are in Birmingham."

"So, pick another course."

I try to breathe through my annoyance. I wanted to have all my information ready before I told my dad about my plans. I know how his mind works, and I know how to work him. Now, he's had time to digest this news and build his arguments against it. He's never going to listen.

"I don't want to pick another," I grumble.

"I don't know why you're so focused on your education anyway. You don't need to study, Skye. You'll be taken care of for the rest of your life."

I don't doubt that. My father is rich beyond what most people can contemplate. The house here is only one of his properties. I know he has at least another two in Birmingham city centre, probably others.

Everything around me was bought with money earned from the blood of others.

"It's not about earning money, Dad."

"So, what's it about?"

I blow out a breath, making a dark lock of hair move out of my eyeline. "It's about carving a path for myself. I can't sit around for the rest of my life doing nothing."

"That's not going to happen anyway. At some point, you'll have kids and a husband."

I huff out a derisive laugh. "So, I'm just reduced to being a nineteen-fifties stereotype?"

"You don't want kids and a family of your own?"

In truth, I haven't thought that far ahead. I'm barely eighteen. I want to live my life. I'd love to travel and see the world, but I'm pretty sure my father will never let me have my passport. "Maybe. But right now? No. I want to do something though."

"So, find a hobby."

I close my eyes and ask the universe for strength. "It's easy for you. This was always your path. I don't know what I'm meant to do with my life. You've made it clear I'm not a part of your world and that I have no place in it, but you won't allow me to be a part of the civilian world either, so where does that leave me? I need to have a life, Dad."

He stands, wiping his hands on his pants as he does. "You have a life. Here."

"I have a cage," I snap, losing control of my emotions.

Glancing around at the expensive cabinets and appliances that fill the kitchen, he frowns. "If you think this is a cage, I worry about you."

"You're twisting everything I'm saying."

"So, it's not a cage?"

I've never contemplated patricide as much as I am in this moment. "Do you mean to keep me here forever?"

I hold my breath, scared to know this answer. I don't want to be a prisoner in my own life, but that's seeming more likely. My father doesn't want to let go of the reins even a little.

"I told you to pick a university."

"But only if it's in the city." Oh yeah, the bitterness is unmistakable, and I can't stop it from slipping out.

"Do you know what would happen to you if one of my enemies got hold of you?"

I swallow down the sudden unease creeping up my throat. "No one is going to take me."

"Really? You know that for sure, do you?" He leans on the table, his face moving so it's in mine. "You get to sleep easy in your bed night after night feeling safe and secure because I've made it that way for you, Skye. You don't lie awake wondering if today will be the day that someone snatches your daughter and does things to her that can't be undone. Rape, mutilation, horrors that you can't even imagine… there are so many things that could happen to you if I don't put these measures into place. So, yeah, you might feel like you're in a cage, but you're sitting in front of me happy and healthy, so I can live with that."

Despite the harshness of his tone, he moves positions so he can kiss the top of my head. Shivers run along my spine, and the fine hairs on my arms stand up as his words fill me with a dread like I've never felt before. What's going on? Dad's always had enemies, but he's never told me that he worries about me being raped by them.

"Stop trying to scare me," I accuse in a small voice.

"You should be scared, sweetheart. You're a woman now, and the reality is everywhere you go, that fact will be used against you." He grabs his mobile phone off the tabletop and slips it into the inside pocket of his brown leather jacket. "You can go anywhere you want as long as it's within Pioneers territory."

He gives me a final glance before he leaves me sitting alone at the table, feeling as if he has thoroughly clipped my wings.

"You know what you need?"

I focus on the ceiling above my head, tracing the swirling patterns in the Artex. For the past week, my mind has been full of the conversation I had with my father at the kitchen table.

I never really considered my life might be in danger. I know my dad's lifestyle is deadly, but the bubble he's built around me has given me a false sense of security. That realisation has been in my thoughts constantly.

Am I safe?

Will I ever be able to have a normal life?

In some ways, I hate Scarlett for that. She will never be the target of anyone, even though her father ranks highly in the Pioneers.

"Are you listening?" She throws a teddy at me, hitting me in the side of the head.

"I would if you were saying anything interesting," I jest, tossing it back.

She snatches it out of the air and clings to it like it's a safety blanket.

"Bitch."

I laugh, draping my hand over my eyes to block out the light from my bedside lamp. I've had the same bedroom since I was six years old, and even though the colour has changed over the years, I feel at home in the space. Could I really move out?

Even if it's only into the city centre?

"Cow," I banter back.

"What's going on with you?" she asks, sitting up. "You've been quiet all week, but tonight, you're boring the shit out of me."

I move my arm enough so I can glare at her. "Thanks."

"I'm serious, Skye. You're acting like the world ended."

I sit up slowly, wondering if I should even say anything. Outside of Tommy, Scarlett is my closest friend, but she isn't going to understand. She's never been restricted in the same ways I am.

I thought eighteen would release the hold my father has over me, but he's made it clear that's never going to happen. He has control over everything in my life, including the people in it.

Dad indulged my friendship with Tommy because it served a purpose, but his absence from my life tells me everything. Don't question the great Desmond Richardson. I challenged him, and now, my best friend has vanished. I've messaged and called, but both remain unanswered. I'm being punished for speaking out.

"Have you seen Tommy?"

She frowns. "Um, like two days ago. He came to the house to talk to my dad."

Great. So, it's just me who is being avoided. I try not to let the dismay overwhelm me. "Did he seem okay?"

"He seemed like Tommy. What's going on?"

I pull my bottom lip between my teeth, fighting back the tears. I'm not a crier. It has never been something that was indulged in my house. My body doesn't care, though, and I have to swipe at my cheeks to remove the evidence.

"Hey! What's wrong?" Scarlett scrambles to her knees,

moving to me as I fight back my emotions. "Talk to me, babe."

"I'm tired," I admit. "My dad keeps me like a prized possession and Tommy… he's being pulled into that life more and more. I hate it. I see what it's done to Jack, and I don't want that for Tommy. And Dad found out I'm looking at universities farther away from home and he made it clear I'm not going anywhere outside Birmingham. I just feel trapped, and I can't breathe."

My words rush out, stumbling into each other in my haste to relieve the pressure building within me. I want to say more, but my throat is so tight, I can barely draw in air.

Arms wrap around me, and I'm pulled into Scarlett's embrace. "Take a breath, okay? It's fine. You're fine. Just try to calm down."

I lean against her, sucking up all her strength.

"Let's just deal with this one problem at a time. Tommy'll be fine. He's got his brother to take care of him, and my brothers too."

"It's never going to be the same. He's already changing."

"He's one of them, Skye. A Pioneer. I don't like it either, but it was always going to be the way. This is the life."

I hate her for saying that because I know it's true. "I want things to go back to the way they were."

"I know, but everything changes. Nothing ever stays the same. And I'm glad your dad found out about your plans to move away."

I pull back from her, the burn of betrayal stinging through me. She's meant to be on my side, not his.

"Did you tell him?" I accuse.

Her eyes roll. "Of course not. I would never, and you know that."

I feel bad for accusing her because she's right, she never would break my trust like that.

"Sorry," I say immediately.

"You're fine. You're upset. But I do mean it. You're my best friend, Skye. The only friend I have because my dad is a lunatic, and everyone is scared to talk to me. If you leave, I'll die here."

There is a pit in my stomach as her words settle around me. She's just lonely, like I am, and she's right. We're all each other has. Tommy was never mine to keep. His path was carved from the moment he took his first breath.

"I'm not going anywhere. Dad won't let me."

She falls back onto the bed, the mattress dipping as she does, her blonde hair spread around her head like a halo. "You really want to leave?"

"You don't?"

She considers my question for a moment before shifting her shoulders. "I guess. I don't know. I've never really thought about it."

I don't know how to respond to that without being mean, so when my phone rings on the bedside table, it's almost a relief.

Climbing over the bed, I grab it. Tommy's name flashes up, and I beam as I swipe to answer the call.

"Hey! I was just thinking about—"

"Jack's dead." He cuts through my words like a knife, and the wound he leaves behind is visceral.

"What?"

"He's dead." The bluntness in his delivery stops my brain from immediately understanding what he's saying.

"What do you mean?"

"Some fucking biker club killed him." The strain in his words gores me. I know he shouldn't be divulging any of this information to me, but the way his voice trembles between anger and distress tells me everything. He's breaking.

"Which club? What happened?" I sit up straight, everything feeling wrong. Jack can't be dead.

"The fucking Untamed Sons. *Fuck!*" He snaps out the words like an elastic band pulled too tight. I've heard of the Sons. They're an MC that the Pioneers had problems with. I thought that had been resolved, though. "They cut him down like a dog, left him bleeding to death after murdering Bobby and Finn. They're gonna pay, Skye. Every single one of them. I'm gonna kill them all, even if it takes me the rest of my life. Jack's… he's… *fuck!*"

My breath is lodged in my chest, and my heart is racing. "Don't do anything stupid."

"He's fuckin' gone. He's just *gone*." The way his voice cracks and his emotion pours out hits me in the gut like a wrecking ball. My heart is breaking for him and for Jack. Visions of the boy who used to run around the grounds with us fills my mind. *How can he be dead?*

I try not to think about that. Tommy needs me right now.

"Where are you? I'll come to you."

"No. You stay where you are. Things are gonna get messy." He pauses for a second. "Love you, Skye. Don't ever doubt that. You're my girl. You'll always be my girl."

The line goes dead, and I pull my phone from ear to stare at the screen. The feeling that washes over me is like nothing I've ever felt before. I'm suddenly terrified.

"What's going on?" Scarlett asks, fear in her eyes.

"Jack's… Jack's dead."

And everything is going to change.

CHAPTER 3
RAGE

My skin itches as soon as I step foot outside the police station. For a moment, I let the cooler air wash over me, cleansing the filth away.

I hate those fucking places.

Ain't my first time in a cell, and I doubt it will be my last. I don't just find trouble everywhere I go, I seek it out. There's something about the thrill of releasing the rage that burns inside me. It's more than cathartic—it's necessary. I have to release that shit somehow.

When that prick started on me in the bar last night, I lost it. There was no build-up to my temper, I unleashed it without prelude. Nought to sixty miles per hour in the blink of an eye. One moment, that fuck is giving me shit, the next, he's on the floor bleeding. The anger was never in me, not before my father unleashed his torment. The nonstop torture broke me, and now, there's a dark rage that beats inside me, one that scares even me.

Stretching my back, I tip my head towards the sun, letting the weak heat soak into my skin. Even that small amount of time locked away was enough to unsettle my already dangerous mind.

Kept in a small space like a caged animal with nowhere to escape my own thoughts is hell for someone like me. No one in the club knows my past and the torment I suffered at the hands of my father. No one, not even Ravage, knows that I left him to burn, without feeling even a hint of remorse.

The road beyond the police station is bustling with traffic. Cars, cyclists, and black cabs all fight for their position on the road. It's the rat race that society is forced to participate in. That's why I joined the club. The expectations that exist in the real world do not in this one. But even the club has its own rules, ones that I'm constantly breaking.

I know my President and Vice President are losing their patience with me, but I don't know how else to be. The anger that beats inside me is not something I can control or curtail.

I pause on the steps outside the station and pull out the plastic bag the desk sergeant handed to me before I left. My phone battery is dead, unsurprising. I doubt anyone thought to switch it off after I was arrested. I grab instead the packet of cigarettes, opening the lid and pulling one out. As I slide it between my lips, digging back into the bag for a lighter, I can't help but think if I continue the way I am, I'm not going to see twenty.

Somehow, that's not the deterrent it should be. What

do I care about living a long life? What the fuck do I have to live for anyway? I got nothing but the club.

"Kid."

It ain't my name, but I know it's directed at me. I lift my head in the direction it came from and see my VP, Nox, leaning against the wall to the left of where I'm standing. I don't know how I didn't see him. Nox ain't a small guy, and his shaved head makes him look like the thug he is. We're all animals.

I take a long drag of my cigarette, letting the nicotine fill my system. It does little to take the edge off, but there's not a lot that can.

"Can't decide if you being here is good for me or bad." I blow the smoke out, my skin itching for a different reason this time.

Ravage has been good to me, but I've pushed my luck over the past few months. Warning after warning has been given about my behaviour, and while I have tried to rein in the temper that consumes me daily, I cannot control the darkness that flows within me.

Nox pushes a booted foot off the wall as I approach, his hard eyes watching me.

Sometimes I feel like he knows my darkest secrets, despite the fact there's no one alive who knows what happened in the flat that day.

"Guess that's for you to decide," he says around a smirk.

Fuck. I knew the moment I threw that first punch that I was on borrowed time. Ravage warned me. He told me my temper would get me into trouble, and the way Nox is looking at me tells me I've stepped over the line.

"Am I out?"

Suddenly, I feel naked without my kutte on my back. The police had stripped it off me when I was arrested, and I'd fought like a demon to get it back. No biker allows anyone to remove their colours, not even the pigs.

"Do you want to be?"

Bile coats the back of my throat. "Fuck no."

Nox starts to walk in the direction of the parking area, and I follow after him like a lost puppy. I've experienced fear many times in my life, but this is different. The club gave me something I haven't had for a long time.

Family.

Have I blown it? I'm not ready to walk away, but that choice will not be mine. "You ain't too good at listening, are you, kid?"

I'm not, so I don't bother trying to deny it. The situation I find myself in is a consequence of my actions. It burns through me knowing that I might have ruined things for myself because of a lack of control.

"That fuck started it first. I just finished it." I sound like a twelve-year-old rather than the nineteen-year-old man I am. That makes the anger inside me bubble. "If I'm out, just fucking say. Ain't gonna beg for a seat at the fucking table."

Nox stops walking and turns to face me. I barely register the movement before his hand is wrapped around my throat and I'm pressed against the side of a small red hatchback. My back stings at the force as I hit the metal frame. My immediate reaction is to fight, to throw punches. I have to swallow down the fury building inside me before it gains a stranglehold.

Instead, I try not to focus on the ironclad grasp around my throat and concentrate on meeting the gaze of my Vice President. There's no mistaking the burning anger in his eyes as he stares at me. "You've got potential, Beau. More potential than I've seen in any prospect who has come through our ranks in the past five years. But that fucking hot head of yours undoes everything. Can't go into a situation expecting you to have a brother's back. Not when the slightest inconvenience makes you lose your mind."

He releases his hold on my neck, and I ball my fingers into fists at my sides, gritting my teeth so I don't lash out. "He riled me."

Nox throws his hands up into the air, his frustration clear to see. "Being who we are and what we do, people are always going to come at us like that. You've got to learn to control yourself. We need tough men in this club, not loose cannons."

That bile again is climbing up my throat, choking me. "So, I'll do better."

"Ain't about doing better, kid. Ravage is done giving you chances."

Ice fills my veins. No, this ain't happening. I ain't giving up my place. Not like this. I open my mouth to protest, but Nox holds up a hand. I slam my teeth together, knowing if I speak out, it will only cause more problems.

"You're going to Manchester."

I can't stop my brows from drawing together. I've met a few of the Manchester brothers when they've visited our chapter, but they're not my family. I know I deserve the shit, that I brought this upon myself, but injustice still burns through me. "So, you're just sending me away?"

Fuck, I want to rant, but I say nothing. I shouldn't be surprised. My whole life, I've been a burden to whomever was taking care of me. My parents hated me. The foster carers I was bounced between didn't give a fuck either. This is just another notch, another let-down. I don't know why I'm fucking surprised.

Nox steps in front of me before I can move around him. "Take that look off your face. This ain't about anyone pushing you away or denying you a place in the club. Every single one of us wants you to succeed, but I ain't going to treat you like a kid and feed you lies. You and Rav are just going to continue to butt heads. A change of scenery will do you good. You might even learn a few things from Howler and his boys."

"And if I don't want to go?"

"Ain't asking. You're going."

Motherfucker. I pull out a cigarette, lighting it. Somewhere between the door and Nox putting hands on me, I lost the one I sparked up when I left the station, and my body needs the nicotine calm.

"This ain't just about you clashing with Ravage," Nox says. "Manchester needs bodies. They're in deep with this fucking gang, and we've got to help."

We all know about the Dudley Pioneers and how they

targeted the Manchester chapter after taking on Birmingham. Those fuckers think they can keep coming for our club without any repercussions, they're wrong. So, fighting against them and helping my club brothers feels righteous, but I'm not the best person to send into an already volatile situation.

"It's already a powder keg there. You sure you want to send me?"

Nox blows out a breath, his eyebrows tugging together. "Ain't sure about anything these days, but I got an old lady and a daughter. Most of the brothers in that chapter have families they need to protect. We could use a little of your brand of crazy." The admission is given with a lopsided smile.

It's a compliment, one that should have me grinning like a maniac. I've wanted for so long to find my place in the club, and now, Nox is offering the chance for me to play the hero. So, why does my gut feel hollow?

I want to dig my heels in and refuse, but if Rav wants me to go, then I have to go.

"Fine. But I won't play nice with these cunts. Just putting it out there that I could make the situation worse."

Nox seems to consider my words before he speaks. "I think that ship has sailed, kid. This ain't about rebuilding bridges. The shit they've done can't be fixed. Even if the club tried to, Trick ain't going to stop his rampage, and I don't blame him. He lost the love of his life, and if someone took Lucy or Nora from me… fuck, I'd do exactly what he's doing. But we have to ensure the survival of our Manchester chapter and keep those families safe. You're going to play a part in that, Beau."

My real name on his tongue makes me cringe. I've never liked it, and hearing it takes me back to feeling like that scared kid fighting against my father. Old scars seem to throb even though they're long healed. He can't call me that. "Didn't you hear the boys gave me a road name?"

He smirks, shaking his head. "Heard it, and I can't say it doesn't suit you."

Rage is the one emotion that constantly feeds the beast within me. I know I've got a temper, that I'm quick to anger. That's not a secret, and it's not something I can control. My father killed any sense of control I might have had as an adult. Now, I see danger and I react. Sometimes, I fight because I enjoy the thrill of it. Considering what I went through, I shouldn't enjoy inflicting pain on others, but I do. It takes so little to pull that hair trigger.

"Didn't mean to disrespect you, Rage," Nox adds. "It's gonna take some time to get used to calling you that."

"No hard feelings," I assure him, dropping my cigarette to the ground and crushing it under my boot. "You have my kutte?"

Levi grabbed it when the pigs had taken it from my back, and while I know the brother will have kept it safe, I want it back in my possession.

"It's in the cage. You want to put it on?"

How is that even a question. "Fuck yeah."

I follow as he walks over to a dark blue car I recognise as one of the pool cars the club uses. Most brothers hate driving cages, but at times it's necessary, especially considering the number of old ladies and kids in our chapter. When I was a prospect, I drove the women wherever they needed to go, sometimes the kids too.

Fuck, how the hell am I supposed to walk away from my chapter family?

I don't express the injustice that churns through my gut. There's no point. I made this bed, and now, I have to lie in it. Nox, Titch, hell, even Fury warned me what would happen if I kept playing with fire.

Part of me knew I was on a path of self-destruction, one that led to this moment, but that anger inside me makes me lose all sense of rationality. I'm lucky Rav is even giving me this chance, even if it is two hundred miles from home.

I ignore the feeling of coming out of my skin while Nox opens the back door of the car.

I'm still worthy of the patch.

I'm still a brother.

I cling to that knowledge, refusing to dwell on anything else. Nothing matters but keeping those colours on my back.

When Nox emerges clutching my kutte between his fingers, I almost snatch it from his hands. The nakedness I feel when I'm not wearing it is disarming. It's not just leather but plate armour that protects me from the outside world.

When he holds it out to me, I take it from him, trying not to appear too desperate. Knowing how close I came to losing this, to losing everything, should have me vowing to do better, but I'm not deluded.

I understand better than anyone the man I am.

Shrugging into it, I settle the leather into place. It moulds around my shoulders, fitting like a glove.

"I'll take you back to the clubhouse, give you a chance to say your goodbyes, and then you gotta hit the road. Howler's expecting you."

Fuck, this is happening, and I don't know that I'm ready for it. "When this shit is over with the Pioneers, do I get to come back to London?"

"That's Rav's decision, Rage."

It ain't a no, but it ain't exactly a yes either.

I get into the car, restlessness I've not felt for a long time surging through me. Neither of us speak a word as he drives me back to the clubhouse.

When the building comes into view, all I can think about is leaving the only place that has ever felt like home. Nox stops the car after pulling into a space between a couple of other cages.

I notice the vehicles belonging to the wives and families of some of the brothers. The full row of bikes tells me there's a full house inside, waiting to say their goodbyes.

As I get out the car, I don't move from the passenger side. How the fuck do I handle this? The last thing I want is some tearful ceremony. I don't want to be reminded of what I'm losing.

Nox's eyes bore into the side of my head. "You okay?"

I pull my bottom lip between my teeth, sucking in a breath. I'm not even close to okay, but I'm not telling my Vice President that. "Ain't big on goodbyes. Just going grab my shit and go, if it's all the same to you."

"My old lady ain't going to like that," he says.

I'm pretty sure everyone will be glad to see the back of me, especially Ravage, but I don't say this. "I'm sure you'll make her feel better about the situation."

"You sure this is how you want to play it?"

I nod. "Pack my shit and hit the road."

Nox comes to me, his hand resting on my shoulder as he gives it a forceful squeeze. "This ain't forever."

I smile, but I don't believe his words. I have a sixth sense for knowing when things are going to change in my life, and I'm pretty certain this is one of those moments.

"I mean it, Rage. Give it some time between you and Rav. Do some growing, learn some control, and then come home."

Home...

That's what I thought this place was, but now, I'm not so sure. A home shouldn't be so easily taken from you.

"See you soon, Nox."

He seems as if he wants to say something more, but I don't give him the chance.

As I head into the clubhouse, I hear music coming from the common room. I bypass it, heading instead to the small room that has been my home since I became a patched member of my club.

It's filthy as fuck, with take-out cartons and wrappers littering the top of the dresser. The covers are pooled in the middle of the bed, the sheet pulled out of place exposing the mattress below. This is the first place where I'd ever bothered to unpack my shit. That thought rolls around my brain as I reach into the bottom of the wardrobe and pull out a small rucksack. I don't have a lot of stuff. I never have had. Years of being bounced around foster placements and group homes has conditioned me to pack lightly. It's a habit I've carried through to adulthood.

I stuff the handful of T-shirts and jeans into the bottom of the bag. Underwear and socks follow before I grab my wash bag. I don't have any personal effects. There are no pictures of me with family or friends, no mementos from my life either. They should have given me the road name Ghost.

The last thing into my bag is my phone charger, then I zip it up and sling it over my shoulder. I don't give the room a second glance as I head back down the corridor, past the bustling noise of the common room, and outside to my bike.

One of the brothers must have brought it back after I got arrested, but I take quick moment to scan the paint and bodywork, checking for damage. My girl looks whole, the bumps and bruises to her frame are old injuries. To be in the club, every member must have a bike. I'd come from nothing, and I had nothing, so I bought the cheapest roadworthy motorcycle I could find. My plan is to upgrade in the next few years, as I start earning more within the club, providing I can keep my temper long enough to keep my kutte on my back.

I take a final glance at the clubhouse before I pull on my helmet and start up the bike.

Letting my mind empty, I ride out of London and hit the motorway north. As I pass Birmingham, it starts to rain, and by the time I reach the Ancoats area of the city, I'm soaked to the bone.

The club's Manchester chapter sits down a cul-de-sac, away from the bustling life and soul of the city centre. As I pull onto the road, I see lines of bikes parked up either side of the street.

I roam my bike into the nearest space and kick down the stand, trying to ignore the rivulets of water careening over the metal. Despite the downpour, I take a moment to stretch my legs out as I climb off the bike. My skin feels clammy, my clothes heavy and sodden. That's the only reason I unbuckle my saddlebag to pull out my rucksack. Slinging it over my shoulder, I step up onto the kerb and make my way to the door that leads into the clubhouse.

Standing just inside the frame, out of the pouring rain, is a guy about my age. A prospect. He doesn't have the patches that make him a full brother. I don't recognise him from previous visits, but that ain't unusual. Prospect turnover is pretty fast in this life. Not everyone is cut out to wear the Sons logo on their back.

I pull my helmet off, clutching it between my fingers as water drips from it onto the floor.

The guy in front of me eyes me for a moment. "Howler's expecting you. He'll be in the common room."

Great. I wonder what kind of welcome I'll get here. I'm suddenly fifteen years old, being shunted around different homes, unwanted by everyone. My chest feels tight as I step around the prospect and make my way through the corridor that leads to the common room.

The layout is different from the London clubhouse,

the hallways narrower because of the style of the building. There is no music playing, though I hear the rumble of voices as I get closer.

Pushing through the door, I step into the common room, my eyes instantly scanning the space. There are a few members sitting at tables, or standing at the bar, enjoying a drink.

I ignore all of them, my gaze locking on Howler, who is sitting alone. The distant look in his eyes tells me he's lost in thought, so I approach slowly.

A few brothers watch me as I pass, lifting their chins in acknowledgement, but there is no red carpet rollout for me. The mood in here feels like a wake.

My skin prickles along the back of my neck as I stop at the side of the table where Howler is sitting. I'm drenched, and a puddle gathers beneath my feet, but I don't sit. Howler lifts his eyes to meet mine, and I swear he's aged ten years since I last saw him.

"Welcome to Manchester," he says after a moment.

"Am I welcome?" I can't stop the question from slipping out.

"As long as you're loyal to the patch, to your club brothers, and to me, then yeah, you're welcome in my home."

Those words soothe the darkness inside me far more than they should. I'm not sure when I became someone who needed approval.

When you joined the Sons.

"Tell me what you need," I say.

Howler scrubs a hand over his face, the stubble

covering his jaw close to becoming a full-blown beard. "I need you to prove why they call you Rage."

A smirk plays on my lips. I thought being sent here was punishment to keep me in line, and perhaps that was the case, but the mood in this room tells me things are not going well for my Manchester brothers.

I am more than happy to play the role they want me to.

CHAPTER 4
SKYE

"What do you think is going on?"

I don't turn to face Scarlett; I can't. I'm a Richardson, and we don't show emotion, but if I look at her, I'll break down. Tears already prick my eyes, burning like acid, and my throat feels clogged with a mix of despair and terror.

For weeks now, we've been at the house alone, aside from a handful of guards. I've tried to find out what's going on, but no one will tell me anything, and on the few occasions I've managed to speak to my father, he says nothing. It was as if Jack died and everything changed.

Every week, the body count grows and more Pioneer funerals are held. After the first five, I stopped going, but I know there are services held every week for the fallen.

Tommy told me on the phone that his brother was killed by a motorcycle club. I've told no one I know this apart from Scarlett. Having this information doesn't help me in any way, and I don't want Tommy to get into trouble for something he divulged when he was distraught.

I know Jack's death has hit my friend hard, even if I haven't seen him to verify it. Tommy was close to his brother. He idolised him growing up, always wanting to be like him. I know this will have hit him like a wrecking ball to the gut. Jack may have scared me towards the end, but when I think about him, all I remember is the little kid running around my father's estate, laughing and having fun.

My heart tears into pieces thinking about the lives my father has destroyed. Jack is gone, and Tommy… I don't know what state he's in.

When I don't answer her, she poses the next question. "Have you heard from Tommy or your dad?"

"No." I hate that I'm in the dark with all of this.

My father has never divulged much of his business, and in the past, I never wanted to hear about it anyway. Ignorance is, as they say, bliss, but for the first time in my life, I feel like this has me at a disadvantage.

I don't know what's coming, and that terrifies me.

Gripping the fence tightly, I watch the horses grazing in the field in front of us. It can't ground me, nothing can, but my legs are unsteady enough that I don't trust them if I let go.

"Do you want to ride? It might take your mind off everything."

I appreciate what Scarlett is doing. She's stayed at the house with me from the moment Jack was murdered. I don't know if she's done it out of friendship or if she was told to, but I'm glad she's here. The home I grew up in no longer feels like a sanctuary. I see shadows and darkness in corners that once held happy memories for me.

"No," I say, pushing off the fence.

My legs hold, which gives me the confidence to start walking. The house is in front of me, the red brick stark against the backdrop of greenery. A gravel walkway surrounds the property, plants and shrubs providing splashes of colour, and there's a workshop off to the side that is used to store logs for the burner in the living room.

The sound of a car draws my attention, and instead of heading for the back door, I move around the side of the house. As I approach the driveway in front of the property, I glimpse a dark car that I recognise as one of my father's.

Is he home?

I pick up my pace as the driver's door opens and a familiar figure steps out.

Tommy.

My steps falter and gravel kicks up under my feet as I stutter to a stop. I haven't seen him for so long that everything about him looks different. His hair is longer, and there is a nasty cut running down his cheek that looks fresh. He's not my Tommy. Everything about him is wrong.

Tears sting my eyes.

This is what I was afraid of. Tommy was never built for this life. There is none of the usual humour dancing in his eyes, and when his gaze swings suddenly in my direction, ice fills my veins.

Our eyes meet, locking like magnets onto each other. I want to drag myself away, hide from the coldness that greets me. There is no warmth as he pins me with his hard stare.

Every inch of me feels like flames are licking across my skin. It's as if a match has been struck inside my stomach and it's burning through my gut as I try to find the boy I knew in the beast standing in front of me.

"Tommy…" I whisper his name, willing him to snap out of whatever darkness has claimed him, but he doesn't.

Instead, he rubs his thumb over the base of his nose and strides towards me with a confidence I've never seen from him. This man is a stranger to me, so far removed from the Tommy I knew that I don't recognise a single thing about him.

I brace myself as he comes closer, unsure what I'm scared of, but there is some primal warning light within me that is flashing frantically. Forcing my feet to remain still is a monumental task that costs me the last piece of strength I have remaining.

He stops in front of me, keeping enough distance to respect the barrier I would place between us if I could, and I tip my head back to peer up at him. He's as tall as he's always been, but the way he looms over me makes it feel as if he has gained inches.

"Where are your guards?" he demands, his voice harsh enough to make me flinch.

"What are you doing here?" I ignore his question. I

don't give a shit about my guards. I'm happy to see my best friend, but a dark thought is creeping into my brain. Is he here because something has happened to my dad?

Tommy's brows come together, and despite how much time and distance has come between us, he can still read me like a book. "Your dad's fine," he assures me.

I press a hand to my chest, my heartbeat thrumming so violently, I'm certain I should be able to feel it against my palm. "Where have you been?"

His eyes lift from mine, turning to look away. There isn't a single emotion on his face, but I can sense the rage rolling off him. "Does it matter?"

My mouth moves, but no words burst out of me. *Is he... is he serious?* "I haven't seen you since… since Jack…" I break off, unable to say the word 'died' to Tommy, but he recoils as if I screamed it at him anyway. "Yes, Tommy, it fucking matters."

His jaw clenches. He's holding back the anger he wants to unleash on me, and that feeling of fight or flight flutters in my belly once more. I don't believe Tommy wants to hurt me, not the old Tommy anyway, but I'm not sure about the man in front of me. He's so different, so changed. He has become a Pioneer through and through.

I step back, feeling an unconscious desire to place space between myself and what my instincts perceive as a threat, and his face hardens to granite.

"You scared of me, bug?"

The use of my nickname should soften me, but it only adds to the looming sense of unease rippling through me. "Should I be?"

My words shake, and I hate that they do. I'm not some scared little girl, but in this moment, that's exactly how I feel.

Everything about him turns to stone as he lifts his chin a little. "I'll never hurt you. *Ever*." I don't tell him that he's already hurting me. "Come here."

I want to shake my head, but I also need him, so my feet move of their own accord, and before I can stop myself, I bury my face against his chest. My arms wrap around his body as I tell myself he's who he has always been. He's the boy who I laughed with over the silliest things. He's the boy who woke me in the mornings to make sure I would have a good day.

He's Tommy.

I relax into him, soaking in the faint smell of his aftershave as I hug him tight. Tommy holds me stiffly, as if he has forgotten how to love someone, before his arms wrap around me as well.

The relief I feel being in his arms is indescribable. Every cell in my body relaxes and relents to him.

"Oh shit," he murmurs, his chin resting atop my head. "Fuck, bug. I needed this so badly."

He's not the only one. I let all my fear and all my concerns flow out of me as I'm enveloped in his embrace. It doesn't stop that constant turbulence in my stomach, but it does loosen some of the bands constricting my chest.

"I missed you so much," I admit.

"I missed you too." He nuzzles into my hair, as if he's taking in my smell and committing it to memory. "I don't want to fight with you. I didn't come here to scare you or cause shit."

I pull back from him, scanning his unreadable expression. "Why did you come?"

His tongue dips out to wet his bottom lip as he scrunches his face up a little. "I needed to see you."

This sends a spike of fear through me. There's a finality in his tone that scares me to death. "What's going on? I'm sick of being kept in the dark."

Tommy winces, his chocolate brown eyes closing to half-mast. "I just… I needed to see you." He repeats these words, but I know Tommy, and I know when he's lying. There's more that he's not saying.

"Does my dad know you're here?"

At the mention of my father, he steps back, opening a chasm of space between us. He's suddenly the soldier again, his emotions locked down. "No one does." He forces a smile that remains only on his lips and does not reflect in his eyes as it normally does. "Scarlett driving you crazy yet?"

It's such a normal question, it knocks me off kilter for a moment. "She's been a good friend."

That's a double-edged blade for him, and Tommy takes the cut with a grimace. "I wish I could've been better for you. I wish I had a lifetime to make up my failings to you."

I grab his biceps in a bruising grip as pain clenches my heart. "Don't talk like that! Why are you saying this shit?"

The smile he gives me is genuine, and it knocks the air

from my lungs. "I love you, Skye-bug. Always have. You're my best friend, and I just wanted you to know."

"You're talking like this is the last time you're going to see me."

His laugh is nervous, and it sets all my nerves on fire. "Ain't going anywhere."

"Good, because nothing is going to happen to you."

Even as I say these words, I know they're lies. The world Tommy is a part of now is a dangerous one with short life spans. It's amazing my father has lived this long. As a foot soldier, Tommy's chance of survival is next to zero.

My eyes burn with the need to sob, but I refuse to show that kind of weakness in front of Tommy. I don't think he would accept my tears now.

He shocks me as he grabs my face, cupping it between his rough hands, and forcing my gaze to his.

"Need you to listen to me, and I need you to listen carefully, okay?"

"What?" I whisper the word, terrified out of my mind of what is going to come out of his mouth.

My agreement seems to calm him a little. "If we all fall, you run, bug. You leave Birmingham. You leave the U.K. You get as far away as possible from the Untamed Sons. Do you understand?"

A lump lodges in my throat that I can't breathe around. Everything feels tight and heavy. "I'm not going anywhere without you and my dad."

"You're going to have to. The path I'm on… I don't think there's a way off it for me."

He might as well have speared me in the chest. The pain is physical and makes me gasp. "You're freaking me out," I admit.

"I know."

The way he's looking at me has my panic rising another twenty notches. "Forget all of that. Let's just leave," I tell him desperately. "We'll go right now." I turn away, intending to run into the house to grab my things, but Tommy's fingers latch around my wrist, stopping me.

"I can't."

I search his face, trying to work out why he would come here to tell me he's self-destructing with no way for me to pull him back from it. "Why not?"

"Because of Jack." The softness in his voice is betrayed by the darkness in his eyes.

"Jack's gone, Tommy. You have to live your life."

I pull out of his grip, suddenly wanting distance and clarity from him. "Jack was murdered, and the fucker who did it is still breathing. Ain't letting that slide. He needs to pay for what he did to my brother."

"So, you die to avenge your brother? Are you out of your mind?"

"You've never lost anyone, Skye. Don't stand there judging me for wanting justice."

"I'm not judging you," I snarl, my temper fraying into a thousand strands. "But where does it end? You kill them, they kill you. Everyone dies, and I'm left alone. How is that a good outcome?" I slam the heel of my palm into his chest, and he jolts backwards. "And I have lost someone, which you'd remember if you weren't being such a dick."

I turn, walking away before I punch him in the face. How dare he come here and tell me I don't know how it feels to lose someone? He held me when I cried after my mum passed. He knows how traumatic that shit was for me, how long I grieved her death.

"Skye. Stop."

I don't. I storm towards the house, gravel crunching beneath my feet. Scarlett is watching us from the living room window, her brows drawn together, but I ignore her. All I can focus on is how little Tommy cares about me in all of this. He avenges his brother, possibly dying in the process, and I'm supposed to just pick up the pieces of what's left?

Fuck that.

And fuck him.

My blood heats as anger rolls through me. I want to rage, but I also want to cry, and I won't do that in front of him. Escape is my best option, but he won't even give me that courtesy.

Hands latch onto me, spinning me around. I fight, shoving Tommy back and screaming in his face. I don't know what I'm saying, but the words spilling out are pure frustration.

"Stop!" he yells, grabbing me so hard, I yelp in pain.

"Fuck you, Tommy!" I scream. "Did you come here to say goodbye before you head out on whatever suicide mission you're planning?"

"I told you. I wanted to see you."

I glare at him, letting all my dismay shine through. "Jack is gone, Tommy, and I know it hurts, but he's dead.

You don't have to go down with him. Please, I'm begging you, leave with me."

His gaze slides to the window, where Scarlett is watching us still, and I wish she would go away, so I can talk to Tommy without an audience.

But this is our world—someone is always watching.

And Tommy will never betray whatever vows he has given to my father to fight for him. In this moment, I find myself hating my dad.

"I can't." There's regret in his voice, more than I think he planned on showing.

It doesn't matter. It's a shot to the heart anyway. I thought I could convince him, that our friendship meant more to him than his loyalty to a man who only sees him as an asset.

I rub a hand over my throat, feeling like there is a noose tightening around it. "Whatever, Tommy. Do whatever you want."

"Bug—"

"Don't call me that," I snap. "Go and get yourself killed. Go and be the good little soldier my father expects, but I won't sit here waiting for you to die. I can't."

His fingers skim over his lips as my words sink in. I can see how affected he is by my statement, and I hold my breath, praying he'll change his mind.

"I'm sorry," he says finally. "I wish I could be who you want me to be, but this is me." He raises his arms out at his sides, challenging me to refute him.

"No, Tommy, it's not you. This has never been you, but I can't live your life for you. All I can ask is that you try to keep yourself alive because I can't bear to lose you."

With that parting shot, I walk into the house, leaving him outside. As soon as the door is closed behind me, I collapse against it, and I finally let my tears fall.

CHAPTER 5
RAGE

I peer down the mass of flesh and blood that had once been a living, breathing person. I'm not squeamish. I've seen enough gore in my life and inflicted enough injuries to be immune, but my stomach does twist just a fraction at what I'm seeing.

This is pure, unfiltered butchery. It's not my way. If I'm going to fight, it's always going to be with my fists. I've never been a fan of weapons. The sperm donor used everything imaginable on me, and I don't want to be like that cunt.

What I see is the anger in this attack. I get it more than any brother in this club. That same fire burns through me too, and it can't be doused. The only way to dampen it down is to release it, and that is only a short-term solution—one that leads to me getting into the kind of shit that got me banished to Manchester.

I stare at the body, trying to make sense of what I'm seeing beneath the mess. There are no discernible features left. No teeth, no eyes either, only a crooked smile carved across his cheek… or what's left of it.

"Fuck me." Hawk covers his mouth, as if he's trying to hold back the tidal wave of shit he wants to unleash.

His frustration doesn't surprise me. It's something I've seen among all the brothers when it comes to Trick and his one-man mission to destroy the Dudley Pioneers.

Since I arrived at Manchester, Trick has been the topic of almost all conversations. The brothers want him to come in, so they can help him and also control the violence between us and the Dudley Pioneers, but Trick ain't playing that game. He's kept his distance and continued to rain shit down on those fuckers.

I'm more inclined to side with Trick, even if it puts the rest of us in danger.

"Why are we always ten steps behind him?"

I don't think this question is directed at me. Hawk is just letting off steam, but I answer anyway. "You really want to catch him and stop… this?" I wave in the direction of the body.

Hawk stares at me as if I'm a dumb kid, and maybe I am, but I'm also savvy as fuck when it comes to reading people and situations.

Growing up in foster care, bouncing around from home to home, I learnt this pretty fast. There was no choice. For a teen boy with a bad attitude going through the system, life was tough. Plenty thought they could beat the bad out of me. Plenty tried. All failed.

That shit is engrained in my DNA. My dickhead father

told me so many times I had the devil in me, and he created that monster in me.

"What do you think happens when the Pioneers find yet another one of their men carved up?"

I shift my shoulders. "Let them come at us. I don't know why we're tiptoeing around them in the first place. They started this shit when they killed Trick's old lady."

Mara was pregnant when she was gunned down like a dog. It was a race to save their daughter, who was cut out of her body after she was already dead.

Trick saw it all. He was sitting next to her, covered in his wife's brain matter while he raced to get her to the hospital. He watched the love of his life die and, unsurprisingly, lost his fucking mind.

"Here's a lesson for you, kid." Hawk snaps at me in a way that makes my spine go straight. *Motherfucker*. "Trick's little rampage ain't unwarranted, but the way he's doing it is fucking dangerous. It puts our families at risk, and I'll never be okay with that." He grinds his teeth together. "I've lost too many already. Ain't losing anyone else."

I don't compute his words about losing others. He's not the only one to live through hell. Instead, I'm fuelled by the need to unleash the growing heat within my belly. I don't like being dragged down, especially by another brother.

"I get you're pissed, but I don't think it's too much to ask for some respect around here. You all treat me like I'm some dumb prospect, but I wear a fuckin' patch, just like you."

He tilts his head to the side as he considers me. "You don't think you're acting like a dumb prospect?"

My fingers curl into fists, and before I even consider my actions, I slam my knuckles into Hawk's jaw. The brother doesn't expect it. I can tell by the fact he goes back on a foot, his hand fumbling for the wall behind him to steady his wobbly gait.

The red-hot fury that blazes through his eyes should scare me, but I've faced monsters my entire life, and Hawk doesn't frighten me. I square up to him, ready to fight back if he comes at me, which he does.

"You little fuck—"

He steps towards me, probably intending to feed me a knuckle sandwich, but the door opens and we both freeze in place as Blackjack moves inside. His brows are already drawn together before he lifts his head and reads the room. Our VP ain't stupid. He instantly senses the growing tension between me and Hawk.

"Everything okay?" Blackjack glances between us as I move back, putting some distance between us.

Fuck, fuck, *fuck*.

I'm so screwed.

This'll be my patch for sure.

I swallow the bile working up my throat as I wait for Hawk to rat me out. My heart thuds in my chest and my breath tears out of me as I try to regain control of my turmoiling emotions. I want to live up to my name and rage. I want to break shit to calm the frustration choking me. But I'm balanced on a cunt's hair as it is with the club. As much as I don't want to be exiled to Manchester, I know I have to do my time here if I'm going to have any chance of getting back to London, and that means I need to calm my fucking shit and prove myself. Slugging another brother in the face, especially one as respected as Hawk, ain't the way to do that.

What was I thinking?

You weren't, and that's the fucking problem.

I never engage my brain. I act out before I consider the consequences. That's always been my way. It was how I had to be to protect myself over the years. Here, that shit won't fly. Ravage was sick of my shit. That's why he exiled me here. Now, Howler's going to be forced to do the same.

I steel my spine as Hawk glares at me under heavy lids, the urge to protect myself overwhelming, not from physical damage—I can handle that—but from the emotional blow Hawk has the ability to destroy me with.

One word… that's all it will take.

One word and he could end my time with the club.

Then what?

Where do I go then? Back to couch surfing or staying in hostels? Back to a life alone with no one and nothing? Trying to hold down shit jobs that pay a pittance?

I can't do it. Ain't cut out for the nine-to-five grind, paying bills, being respectable.

But once again, I'm in a situation where I'm staring down a loaded barrel of my own consequences and kicking myself for letting my crazy out of the box.

I stare at the red mark spreading across Hawk's jaw where I hit him. I'd put a lot of weight behind it, so he's no doubt going to bruise there. I wouldn't blame him for slugging me back, but he doesn't move.

"Anyone want to answer?" Blackjack asks when neither of us speaks.

I hold my breath, waiting for the inevitable blow, but Hawk surprises the hell out of me by saying, "Everything's fucking peachy."

My brows automatically draw together. *What the fuck?* I stare at the brother. Why didn't he tell the VP what I did?

I'm not sure Blackjack buys the shit Hawk is peddling, but he doesn't challenge him either. Hawk has earned that respect. As much as it pains me to admit it, I've not.

Not yet.

Blackjack drags his gaze from us and peers at the mangled corpse, his nose wrinkling. "Any idea who the poor bastard staining the concrete is?"

"Nope." Hawk's tight tone makes me wince. He might have kept my shit secret, but that doesn't mean he ain't pissed about it. "You see any sign of Trick?"

"He's long gone." Blackjack huffs out a breath before he scrubs a hand over his thick beard. "I'm getting tired of trailing after him and cleaning up the messes he's making."

Trick is pushing everyone's buttons, except mine.

I live for the chaos.

I shouldn't say shit, but the words slip out before I can stop them. "Did you expect him to wait around for us to find him?"

The Pioneers created the beast Trick has become. We all put the Sons patch on our backs knowing the dangers this life brings, but not old ladies. Never them. It was the first bylaw I was taught when I put my kutte on for the first time.

Don't harm old ladies, and don't steal a brother's woman.

Rules to live by. Rules to die by. This piece of shit gang don't have the same morals we do, and the brothers need to remember that. Mara won't be the only casualty of this war.

Blackjack shakes himself. "He needs to let us handle this as a club. He doesn't have to do this shit alone."

"So you can put a leash on him?" I snort.

Trick ain't going to let that happen. He's not done killing Pioneers. All we can do is try to minimise the fallout.

Or take Trick down ourselves.

That's a thought I'm sure every brother has considered, even if they won't admit it. A lot of the guys have kids and wives to protect.

"We don't want to leash him," Hawk snaps. "We just don't want to fucking bury him in the plot next to Mara."

"There's no way of stopping this now. Even if Trick hangs up his knives and leaves the Pioneers alone. They're going to want revenge for the blood he's shed. They kill us, we kill them back—there's no end to that."

Hawk glances at Blackjack. They all must have come to this same conclusion. I'm not the smartest, but I know people, and I know this ain't ever going to be over for the Pioneers, which means it'll never be over for us.

"This ends when we destroy the Pioneers," Hawk says, "as a club."

"And in the meantime, we do what? Dodge the bullets flying back at us?"

"Trick's made bad decisions," Blackjack admits, "but he's hurting. Ain't a single one of us who wouldn't do the same if we saw what he did. Mara was family to all of us, but he *loved* her. Know you're young, kid, and you ain't ever experienced a love that consuming, but she was everything to him. Trick's a good guy and a great club brother. He's just lost."

I laugh. That's fucking hilarious. They think the guy creating a war between us and the Pioneers is a good fucking guy? I don't know Trick well, but I see the fallout of the shit storm he's created with his actions. "I know our club is built on loyalty, but how much rope are you going to give him to hang himself?"

Hawk's eyes meet mine, steely and resolute, while Blackjack pulls his lips into a snarl.

I should probably shut my mouth, leave my opinions at the door, but I'm a patched brother and I have a stake in this now. My life is as much on the line as any member of this chapter because I wear the Manchester patch on my back.

"Careful," Blackjack growls. "You're skating on thin ice."

I don't heed the warning. "You defend a guy who disrespects the patch and is a shitty father, but I get sent into exile for getting into a bar fight that affected no one except me? What kind of fucked-up logic is that?"

"Don't talk about shit you don't understand," Hawk snaps at me.

"Oh, I understand. The brother lost his wife in a horrific way. I would be doing exactly what he's doing, *if* I didn't have a kid waiting at home for me. Has that baby even seen her dad? She even know he exist?" I know I'm needling them now, but I can't stop. "You guys treat him like he needs to fucking hug this shit out over a beer when he plunged our club into a war that has no end in sight. I'll do what I'm told because that's what wearing the patch means to me, even if it doesn't to him, but don't stand here and tell me that waste of space dickhead is worthy of this unquestioning loyalty from—"

Fingers fist into my kutte and I'm spun around until I'm nose to nose with Blackjack. The darkness in his eyes would be terrifying if I hadn't looked a real demon in the face all those years ago.

"You don't get to insult a man you know nothing about or the way this chapter runs!"

It takes all my strength not to retaliate, not to defend myself. Every instinct in my body urges me to attack. "I know enough."

"Kid, you should just stop talking," Hawk warns.

I barely register his words because all my focus is on my VP, who looks pissed enough to knock out my teeth.

"You've been with us for five fuckin' minutes, Rage. You've met Trick, what, two or three times when you've come through here on runs? You saw him at his fucking best then. I've known that man for years. I know every single thing there is to know about him, including how excited he was to be a father before they—" He breaks off, blowing a breath through his nose. "Mara didn't deserve to die like that. She didn't deserve to never meet her daughter. She didn't deserve to have that child cut out of her while she was taking her last breaths. Trick… he saw all that. He lived through every horrific nightmarish moment of that. He's fucking broken and, yeah, he's out there doing shit no one wants him doing, but the loyalty and the hours he's put into this club earn him that leeway. It doesn't afford you that same luxury. You ain't proven yourself yet."

Fuck, that enrages me. "I ain't proven myself? Been with this club two years and done everything that was asked of me!"

"You think two years buys you that respect?" Blackjack laughs, and I grit my teeth so hard, my jaw hurts. "Wake up, brother." He releases me with a shove before turning to Hawk. "Call in a clean-up."

He doesn't say another word before he storms out the room. Silence lingers between me and Hawk, the air charged with tension as I pull my kutte back into place. The feeling of being worthless, of being nothing, rolls over me, leaving a sticky, unpleasant sensation in my gut.

I stare at the door Blackjack went through, my body wound tight like a coiled spring. I force my feet not to move, even though I want to.

"Whatever shit you're thinking of doing, don't," Hawk warns.

"Ain't doing shit," I mutter.

Hawk pulls out his phone and swipes his fingers over the screen. "Hitting me is one thing. You put a fist in our

VP's face, they'll strip you of your kutte and toss you out on your arse."

I loosen my jaw. "I just said what everyone else is thinking."

He puts his phone away and raises his gaze to me. "No, you didn't. Trick is family. Club family. He earned his place here, and so we're going to do everything we can to bring him home to his daughter and help him be the father that child deserves. If you don't want to get onboard with that, you'd best fuck off back to London." Hawk shakes his head. "That temper of yours… it's going to be your ruin."

He's not saying anything I don't know, so I don't disagree.

"Oh, and Rage? You come at me like that again and I'll feed you your fucking teeth, understand?"

Fuck. "Yeah, I understand."

"Come on. Let's get the fuck out of here."

Giving the corpse a final glance, I turn and follow Hawk out of the building. Blackjack is waiting astride his bike, finishing up a call as we approach.

The Manchester skyline rises around us in the dusk light. It's different from London. The mix of old and new buildings is similar, but I can tell this isn't home. London feels busy and chaotic in a way Manchester doesn't. Older too. I feel like I'm walking in the footprints of a thousand generations in my home city. I don't get that in Manchester, even though there is plenty of history here too.

Sucking in a breath, the fresh air hits my lungs and

chases the smell of stale blood and decomposition from my nose. The urge to light up a cigarette has me reaching for the inside pocket of my kutte, but Blackjack starts up his engine, and Hawk is already moving to his motorcycle.

I guess the smoke will have to wait. My VP is eager to get going.

I climb onto my bike and prepare to ride. We're away from the prying eyes of nosy locals here, but as irritated as I am with everything, I still scan the landscape. There are dangers being outside the protection of the club, and neither my VP nor another brother are dying on my watch.

I give the building a final glance, wondering what Trick was doing here. We're at the back of an industrial estate, the nearest warehouses abandoned long ago. This building looks like it was once an old mill, something the area is famous for. The red brickwork everywhere in this city is crumbling, and the large arched windows positioned at regular intervals have been boarded up to protect the glazing below.

It hasn't stopped the tags covering the plywood.

That's one thing Manchester shares with London. Graffiti is everywhere, and I'm starting to recognise specific tags and designs. These look fresh, and that makes me wonder if the kids doing them are going inside the building. If they do that, they'll find Trick's handiwork, and that opens the club and him to scrutiny.

None of us want that.

I start up my motorcycle and the familiar sound of

rumbling Harley pipes fills the air. I follow after my brothers, keeping close but giving enough space between us to ensure we all stay safe as our headlights cut a path through the growing darkness.

As we hit the main road, I'm conscious of the traffic, making sure to carve a path in front of the cages to keep us all safe. Blackjack didn't tell me where we were going, but from the roads he takes, I know we're heading in the direction of the clubhouse.

The roads that lead to the clubhouse are smaller side streets, even though we're still in the heart of the city. I keep my wits about me, knowing that an ambush could come at any moment.

I'm already alert when something is tossed out in front of Blackjack. It takes my brain a moment to realise it's a stinger—like the shit the police use to stop cars during chases. My VP is too close and doesn't have time to register what it is before he hits it.

That crap people say about everything happening in slow motion is bullshit. This is over in an instant. The scream of metal as Blackjack's bike fishtails before it goes down is loud in the otherwise silent streets. Hawk skids to the side, trying to avoid hitting the spikes, but can do nothing. He's too close, and like Blackjack, the back end of his motorcycle fishtails before it's laid down.

Instinct kicks in, experience riding for the past two years giving me the tools I need to protect myself, but as fast as I react, it's not enough. I twist my handlebars savagely to the right as I apply the brakes. There's nowhere to swerve out of the way because cars line either side of the road, so all I can do is brace as I impact the spikes.

The bike jolts as it hits, and I instantly lose control. The back end spins out before me, and my bike go down heavily. I feel the scraping of the tarmac beneath me through my jeans as I slide across the ground. Pain claws up my side, radiating through my hip and into my chest before there is a sound of crashing metal.

This whole thing takes less than five seconds. As I come to a stop, the energy that propelled me from the bike losing steam, I lie stunned.

At first, there is no pain, but then it hits. A fiery ache spreads like wildfire up my side, radiating through my hips and down my legs. I try to suck in a breath, but there is so much tightness in my chest that I can't draw it in.

I have to move. I need to make sure Hawk and Blackjack are protected, but my body urges me to remain still until I've taken stock of my injuries. My brain doesn't listen. Groaning, I come up onto my elbows and scan the street.

A car alarm is blaring, the orange lights from the vehicle flashing persistently, illuminating the street. The back tyre of one of the bikes is rotating in a slow motion farther up the street. I can see something bulky lying in the road in front of it, the Sons insignia on its back telling me it's one of my brothers.

Fumbling to get my hands under me, I manage to get my knees. My body hurts, but I'm moving, which tells me nothing is damaged irreparably.

I drag my helmet off my head, ignoring the stabbing

pain that radiates from the base of my spine up to my shoulders. My body should be flooded with adrenaline, with fear, but there's a calm that beats inside me as I stumble to my feet.

Two figures step out from behind a car, their hands loose at their sides and clutching machetes. I don't recognise either of them, but I don't need to. The club only has one enemy right now.

The Dudley Pioneers.

I realise the brother lying on the road is Blackjack. I don't see Hawk, which quickens my pulse.

There isn't time to dwell on that. I have to protect my brothers, and myself. I drag my knife out of the sheath on my belt. It's a fraction the size of the ones these men are wielding, but that will not stop me from fighting.

The familiar rage starts to bubble in the centre of my chest as they come towards me.

Where the fuck is Hawk?

I could use his help, but I'll fight either way. Hand-to-hand, face-to-face is my favourite kind of altercation. I know the smile on my face is maniacal as I rush them. There's a split second of panic as they realise their weapons don't scare me, then they're ready to engage.

I feel the blade of the nearest attacker's weapon slice through the tough skin of my arm. The pain barely registers as I give him a sinister grin.

They both come at me, hard and fast, but I have years of fighting dirty behind me. Despite having my body rattled by the crash, I rely on instinct to fight back.

I unleash, letting the anger and the poison that builds

inside me every day out of the box. There is no thought, no consideration of anything besides destroying the men who pose a threat.

Violence flows freely as I grab the nearest man's wrist before he can bring the machete down in a sweeping motion that would slice through my shoulder if I'd allowed it.

With my other hand, I slam the heel of it up and against his nose. Blood sprays in every direction, hitting my skin too, but I ignore it. With unbridled fury, I slam my fist into his gut, making him retch.

The other man tries to attack me from the side, intending to help his friend, but I've been brawling for so many years and taken so many punches, I notice his approach before his machete can find a target.

Red films my eyes, not blood but that uncontrolled hatred that I feel every time someone tries to harm me. In this moment, I'm facing the monster that shaped me into who I am now. My father thought I was the devil, but it was him who planted that evil within me.

Still gripping the man's wrist, I use all my strength to bring the machete down and slice it through the new attacker's side. The man screams, a sound so terrible it should curdle the blood in my veins, but it only serves to push me harder.

Controlling his arm, I force the machete farther into the soft flesh, relishing the noises coming from the other man.

"Stop!" he begs, smacking the back of my head with his free hand.

I don't listen. I drag the wrist holding the machete out of his body, and with my other hand, I shove him back. His knees fold like tissue paper and he falls back against the tarmac. His shirt is soaked, crimson staining the light material.

When I turn back to the other man, his eyes are wide with fear. I squeeze his wrist until he loosens his grip enough for me to take the machete from him.

He knows he's done for, but I ignore his pleas. He let me free when he attacked, and now, he's going to experience the reasons why my London brothers named me Rage.

I hack at him, his screams ringing in my ears and drawing a maniacal laugh from me. Blood sprays up my face, in my mouth until I can taste it, and still I attack. My arm aches with each swing of the blade, and when I bring it down over and over, there are moments where I have to use my foot to free it from the bone.

The man is no longer moving, his silence annoying. I want to hear him suffer. I want him to know the power I wield against those who try to hurt me. My hands are sticky and slippery as I release the machete, using my fists instead as I roar at him. This isn't about dying or about protection. The dam that was holding back my feelings about being abandoned by London is broken, and my emotions are a tsunami.

I'm so lost, too far gone to rein myself back in, and I don't want to. The desire to cause as much suffering as possible consumes me almost completely.

"Rage! He's gone. Stop!"

The voice barely penetrates. I'm too focused on letting all that tension out of my body.

"Fuck! Sorry, brother. This is for your own good."

I turn just barely in time to see Hawk's fist coming towards my face. Pain blasts through my temple, and then, as if someone has turned the lights out, my vision winks out.

CHAPTER 6
RAGE

The pain in my head is the first thing I register as I wake. Sharp, stabbing throbs lance through my temple, as if I've had a skinful, but I don't remember drinking.

It wouldn't be the first time I got blackout drunk though. It's the quickest and easiest way to block out my past memories. And there's plenty I don't want to remember.

Scrunching my forehead, I prise my eyes open. Hazy shapes form in my vision, blurred colours all morphing together in a confusing way.

I blink, trying to see more clearly, and the room comes into focus after a moment.

I'm in the common room.

I peer up at the dirty ceiling above as hushed voices murmur around me like the sound of waves crashing against the rocks.

What are they discussing?

It takes my addled brain a moment to recognise the backs of the men standing across the room from where I'm lying. Howler, Hawk, Socket, and Brewer. There's no sign of Terror or Blackjack.

I realise the VP is lying close to me on the floor, his head turned to the side, his eyes closed. There's blood caked on his face, like someone painted red from his hairline down to his jaw.

Fuck, is he... is he dead?

My eyes lock on his chest, the bulk of his kutte and shirt making it hard to tell if he's breathing. My own lungs seize as I watch through blurry vision until his rib cage moves a little.

I swallow back the panic that had been growing in my chest. Losing a club brother would destroy the chapter and probably get me exiled to Siberia.

Without my club colours.

"He's awake," someone says. I think it's Brewer, but there's a faint ringing in my ears that's making it hard to hear.

Ignoring the pain in my body, I struggle into a sitting position. My sight wobbles, and I have to shutter my eyes to stop from passing out, but it stabilises quick enough.

"Lie down," Socket says, reaching my side and trying to push my shoulders back.

I don't let him, instead focusing on the blood coating me. It stains my clothes, the leather of my kutte, and my hands. There are thick deposits under my nails too.

I'd hacked him to pieces.

I remember every moment of the attack, remember

the unbridled anger that had swirled through me, and how I'd taken that out on the fuck in front of me.

I wait for the guilt and remorse to hit me, but it doesn't. I feel nothing.

It's not the first time I've stolen a life, but that was the most brutal way I've ever done it. I'd lost control. I'd acted without any thought of the repercussions or danger I could've brought on the club.

The exact shit that Ravage was always on my back about.

Fuck.

That level of anger got me booted out of the London chapter. Is that what's going to happen now? Is Howler going to cut me loose too?

What happens to me if that is what he decides?

A tendril of ice works through my veins. Yet again, I'm staring down the barrel of a loaded gun, waiting to take a bullet. Coming to Manchester wasn't my choice, but I figured I'd last longer than this.

I'd killed men on the street. In front of houses. In front of civilians. I know where this path leads. I'm on borrowed time as it is, and now, I've created a shit storm that could bring heat to the club.

Howler ain't going to keep me here. I lock eyes with him and meet his hard, steely gaze.

Why doesn't he just tell me I'm gone?

Fuck that. I'm not waiting to be pushed. I'll jump first before I allow that to happen. I'll never beg for a seat at the table, no matter how badly I want to sit at it.

"I'll go and grab my shit." My voice is tight, my heart

racing as I say the words. I don't want to leave, but yet again, my shitty decisions and temper has led to this.

I never learn.

I get my hands under me and struggle to my knees before lurching to my feet. Socket steadies me. "Easy, brother."

Brother...

That word sticks in my throat in a way that makes it hard to breathe. That's all I've ever wanted to hear—that I'm part of this club. Yet it doesn't resonate with me in the way I expect. I still feel hollow inside, and that's because of the way Howler is staring at me. I tear my arm from Socket's grasp, unable to bear his touch on me. He holds up his hands defensively.

"You going somewhere?" Howler asks.

"You want me gone, right?" I hate how sullen I sound, but I'm having to keep a tight hold on my emotions so I don't lash out. "I fucked up."

I hate the way everyone is staring at me, but I focus only on Howler. As President, his voice is the only one that counts in this moment.

"You saved two brothers. You did exactly what you're meant to do, Rage. You protected your club, but that temper of yours…" He breaks off, running his hand over his jaw. "That shit can't happen like that again. Where it happened, it was on our patch, around civilians we have in our pockets. We were able to protect you—this time—but that ain't the case out there. You've got to rein that shit in."

My teeth grind together as I let his words sink in. "This is who I am," I say. "Ain't no changing that."

"Ain't wanting you to change," he counters. "Just want you to be sensible when you're letting off." He grips my shoulder. "You've got fuckin' potential, Rage. The loyalty, the willingness to walk into hell to protect your brothers, that's the shit I want from all my boys. But right now, you're a danger to everyone around you. You've got to learn to control yourself."

"I don't understand." Admitting that kills me, but it's the truth, and I need to know what the hell I'm dealing with. "You want me to be me but not me?"

"I told you when you got here that I needed you to prove why they call you Rage. I meant that. This war ain't one with rules, and to win, we're going to have to play dirty." His hand comes to my shoulder, squeezing it tight. "You're exactly what I need in my club, but I have to know that when I send you out there with one of my boys, you're not going to lose your shit and endanger them. I need to know everyone is coming home to their old ladies, to their families. Ain't sure you're in a place to ensure that just yet."

"What if I can never control it?"

I've tried a lot over the years to calm my shit down, but when I enter that space, that blinding rage, it consumes me. I can't come back from it.

"You can and you will. You have to if you want to keep wearing that kutte."

Howler wanders away and my gut twists.

I don't like ultimatums, never have, but once again, I'm

in this situation where my temper overruled the consequences.

"You're thinking too hard," Hawk says from the side of me.

I turn to him, my brows coming together. "Good thing I can think after you knocked me out."

He makes a noise in the back of his throat that sounds suspiciously like a snort. "How *is* your head?"

"How do you think it is?"

"You didn't leave me much choice. You were gone. I wasn't sure I could bring you out of it."

He doesn't offer an apology. *Fucking prick.*

I pull my lips into a snarl. "You think I'm just some dumb kid with anger issues?"

"You ain't doing much to disprove that right now."

"The double standards here are unbelievable. Trick is running around murdering Pioneers at will. I kill two men who came for us—most likely because of what he's been doing—and I'm the one who needs a time-out? Make it make sense."

Hawk's jaw locks. "Is there a chance you're going to take that huge chip you're carrying off your fuckin' shoulder any time soon?"

I square up to him. Covered in blood, my skin ripped raw from the crash, and my body hurting, I'll fight him.

"What the fuck did you say?"

Hawk doesn't back down. He meets my anger with a calm that infuriates me. "Are you done?"

I narrow my eyes at him. "Fuck off."

His expression doesn't change. No flinch, no flicker of

anger. I feel the other men move closer though, Socket especially.

"Lose the attitude, kid. You ain't going to get far in this club with it."

"I saved your arse, and you're all looking at me like I'm a piece of shit. I didn't put those fucking machete-wielding lunatics in our path."

"No, you didn't."

His agreement, for some reason, pisses me off more than if he had fought against my words. "Then why am I getting shit but he isn't?"

"You think Trick is getting away with any of this?" Socket snorts before adding, "That boy is going to have years of amends to make for this shit."

That surprises me. I didn't get that impression.

"We're not the enemy, kid," Hawk says in a soft voice.

I glance at him, unsure what the hell to make of everything that's being said.

"We need that anger, Rage, but not within the clubhouse. You direct that shit at our enemies, not at your brothers. What you did was crazy as fuck, but you kept us safe. Ain't a single person in this room who ain't grateful for that," Hawk says. "That's what it means to be a brother, Rage. Not fighting with us, not losing your shit every time someone looks at you wrong. It's fighting for the patch, for the club, for the men who will take a bullet for you. You learn to direct that fury in the right places, and you'll go far."

Fuck. I release the tension in my jaw and soften my expression. "You still punched me."

Hawk's mouth tugs at the corners. "I thought you were gonna turn those big blades on me. You were so lost in the anger. I did what I had to, Rage, to keep you safe and me."

That isn't a lie. I don't want to think I would've attacked him, but the truth is, I don't know how it would've played out. When I get into those states, I have no control over myself. It's like a switch is flipped.

"What's wrong with Blackjack?" I ask.

"Ain't sure. He woke up while we were moving him inside, but he's been in and out since." Socket glances over at our VP, his brow furrowed in concern.

"Go take a shower," Hawk says. "Bag your clothes and bring them to me. I'll make sure they're disposed of."

"And the fuckers I killed?"

The two men exchange a look before Socket says, "Taken care of."

My brows draw tighter together. "I killed them in the middle of the street. There's gonna be witnesses in those houses—"

"We have an understanding with the residents and with the police," Hawk interrupts. "Locals won't say shit, and by the time it's been cleaned up, ain't no one ever gonna know what happened anyway."

I don't know why this information surprises me. London had a similar set-up, but I didn't expect to be protected by these men. I was forced upon them, and it's obvious I don't fit in.

"Shower," Hawk says again.

I don't want to, but I leave the common room and head to the room I've been staying in since I arrived from London. My thoughts are in turmoil. My emotions too.

I take my time showering, sluicing the blood from my skin and scrubbing myself until I feel raw. Only then do I step out of the cubicle, grabbing a towel from the rail to wrap around my hips.

Dressing feels like a chore, but I pull on clean clothes, placing my soiled ones in a plastic bag I had in the bottom of the wardrobe.

Wiping the blood from my kutte takes longer than I expect. The leather is soft where it has moulded to my body after so much wear, and flakes have dried in the cracks. I meticulously clean every inch of the garment, ensuring no evidence is left behind, though I'm not certain how it would hold up under the scrutiny of modern science.

By the time I dress and re-enter the common room, Blackjack is conscious and sitting on one of the sofas pushed against the wall. There's an older man standing in front of him, a stethoscope wrapped around his neck and a stoic look on his face.

Blackjack's old lady, Elyse, is sitting next to him, her face a mask of worry as she clutches his hand.

"He okay?" I ask Terror, who is standing near the door.

The brother is massive and imposing. His shaved head is covered in tattoos, and there's a dark look in his eyes that no doubt earned him his road name. The room seems busier, more brothers filling the space than earlier. Reinforcements in case those Pioneer fucks come at us again.

"Doc wants him to go in and get checked over, just to be safe." His gaze goes over his shoulder to Blackjack before coming back to me. "He's pretty beat up after the crash." Terror stares at me for a beat. "I know everyone is giving you shit about what you did, but I just wanted to say I would have done the same. I wouldn't have given two fucks who saw me either."

I raise my brow. "You would?"

"Kid, this ain't a game. One wrong move and the only outcome is the grave. I don't want to lose anyone in this fucking club, so yeah, you do whatever it takes to protect anyone in this club. We ain't blood, but the Sons is family. We take care of family. Always."

Shit. I didn't expect that kind of endorsement from Terror, but I'm also not surprised. He has a lot at stake in this game too. All the brothers in this club do, thanks to the endless numbers of kids and old ladies.

What I want to say back dies on my tongue as Elyse is suddenly at my side. Her eyes are wild, but there's a grimness in them too. I brace myself, wondering what the fuck is about to spill out of her mouth as she peers up at me.

"Thank you."

What the...

"For what?"

"Hawk said you were with them when the... incident happened. He said you protected them both."

I'm surprised he would have said any of that. "I didn't do—"

Before I can say anything, she throws her arms around me and hugs me in a way I've never been embraced. The warmth of her body against me is foreign, and I'm not sure what the hell to do with my hands, so I leave them loose at my sides. It goes on for what feels like an eternity before she pulls back, her eyes swimming with unfallen tears.

"I don't know what I'd do if I lost him. If you ever need anything…" She trails off, her cheeks suddenly flushing, as if she's remembered where we are and who I am. "Anyway… thank you."

I watch her turn and walk back over to her old man, my brows drawn together.

"Smart move getting the old ladies on side," Terror says from my side.

I forgot he was there, and when I slide my eyes towards him, there's a deep smirk on his lips. "At least she appreciates what I did," I say, uncomfortable as hell with this shit.

Terror opens his mouth to retort back at my barb, but before he can, Howler is there. His gaze roams over me, scrutinising in a way that makes me want to shift on my feet even more. "You got your dirty clothes?"

I raise the bag I'm clutching, and he takes it from me. "Need you to do something for me."

Terror pushes off the wall. "That's my cue to disappear."

Howler waits until he's vanished before he speaks again. "I need you to go to Birmingham."

Fuck that. Instantly, my irritation burns. I fucked up, and now, Howler wants to ship me off to Birmingham?

"You want me out the way," I accuse in a flat tone.

"Did I say that?"

"No, but you don't have to. It's obvious."

Howler blows out a breath. "I know you think everyone is out to get you, but that ain't the case. I want you to fit in here, Rage. I think you have potential to be one hell of a brother, but there's a lot of shit you need to work on to get there. Firstly, that temper of yours. I like your fire, brother, but you've got to learn to control how it burns. Secondly, you need to understand that everyone here wants you to succeed. I know you're looking at this as a punishment, but that couldn't be further from the truth. I want you to do this because I trust you to be careful, fast, and be able to deal with anything. Birmingham is Pioneers territory."

I take the compliment as it is intended, letting some of the emotion I'm feeling drain out of me. "I'm going alone?"

"No, Ralph'll go with you."

He's one of the chapter's prospects and a solid guy. Kind of quiet but dependable, from what I've seen.

"What am I doing in Birmingham?" I ask.

Howler stares at me for a beat, then says, "Collecting guns."

CHAPTER 7
SKYE

The gardens are in full bloom. Pretty bursts of colour create a sea of brightness against the gloomy grey sky. I can see the horses grazing in the pasture in the distance, and my heart squeezes.

What happens to them if we're all dead?

It's a horrid, dark thought, and I hate that it creeps into my mind, though it's not the first one to hit me. Lately, my mind and my dreams have been filled with horrors. My thoughts are troubled, and nothing is easing them.

"You're going to get wrinkles if you keep frowning so much," Scarlett warns me.

I don't turn to face her as she moves around the kitchen behind me. The rustling and clinking of ceramics is oddly soothing. I don't think I would have lasted this long in this big house without Scarlett. I owe her so much. She has truly been an amazing friend since my father and Tommy abandoned me, but despite her attempts to take my mind off what's going on, there is a constant tightness in my gut.

"I'll just Botox them out," I mumble.

Scarlett snorts. "You're in a funny mood this morning."

"Sorry. I'm just… worried."

A hand on my arm has me twisting to face the woman who is becoming my closest friend. I never thought anyone could take the spot Tommy occupied for so much of my life, but he's gone and I'm here, trying to survive as best as I can.

"You can't worry about them every moment of the day, Skye. You have to try to live your own life and enjoy it."

She's right. I know this, and I've told myself this more times than I can count, but some days, like this morning, I can't stop the dark clouds from creeping in.

"I'm trying."

Scarlett's perfectly styled loose blonde curls are so pretty. She's so put together. My light brown hair would usually be in a similar fashion, but I've scraped it back into a ponytail.

"I know."

My gaze moves to the window. "Have you noticed it's kind of quiet today?"

"What do you mean?"

"I've been up for about an hour and I haven't seen any guards."

I peer out, as if they will be standing on the other side of the glass, but all I see are plants and trees against the backdrop of a perfectly manicured lawn.

The number of men at the house has dwindled significantly over the past few weeks, but there's always been someone here.

Scarlett remains quiet, so I turn to face her. "What?"

"You haven't seen anyone because we're alone here," she says.

My head snaps in her direction, my heart thudding. "What are you talking about?"

There's a little flash of something across her face that no one else would be able to read, but I've known Scarlett her entire life. I see the guilt for what it is.

"Desmond recalled everyone last night."

"How do you know that?" I demand, giving her my full attention.

Her gaze darts around as her face screws up into a wince. "Michael told me."

The flaring of my eyes probably looks comical, but I'm stunned. "You've been talking to your brother?"

This is the first I'm hearing about this, and my stomach suddenly feels heavy. Why has she kept this from me? "He's… worried about me. About us."

Her brother is twenty-one and a low-level soldier in my father's organisation. He will rise through the ranks in time, becoming one of my father's most trusted men. His name, his family's legacy, assures it.

That Scarlett has kept this from me causes an ugly feeling to slither through me. It's not quite betrayal, but it's close enough. Scarlett is the one person I have left who hasn't screwed me over.

Until now.

"Don't look at me like that," she pleads. "I didn't think.

Nothing was really said. You know I would've told you anything that was important. He was just checking in with us."

I want to believe that, but trust is not something that can easily be repaired after it's broken. "But you decided what was important without asking me."

Her face falls, the crestfallen look spearing my chest. "I would never do anything to hurt you, Skye. We're not blood, but you are my sister."

I try to push down the anger swirling inside me. Scarlett isn't my enemy. She has given up her own life to stay in this prison of marble and chandeliers. I've been so wrapped up in my own fears that I never stopped to consider she might also be terrified for her own family.

"I'm sorry. I've been so self-absorbed. Is your brother okay? What about your dad?"

"They're both okay. Michael has barely told me anything. He checks in and that's it, but last night… he was… different. He seemed worried, and I don't want to say it, but he was scared."

My blood feels sluggish in its attempt to beat around my body. "Do you think they're in danger?"

"Skye, they've been in danger from the moment they joined the Pioneers. Every day they step out the door is a risk."

That's true, and it scares me.

I pull her into my arms for a hug, needing to be connected and to reassure myself. Scarlett holds me tight, like she's terrified to let go.

"If my dad recalled everyone, that means trouble," I say

softly. I don't want to scare her, but Scarlett isn't stupid either. She knows this.

"Right," she agrees. "He wouldn't leave you here alone undefended unless it was something bad."

It's all been bad. The deaths have piled up in the past month, and men I grew up with as uncles are gone. Soldiers who often came to the house with my dad too. I've stopped paying attention to the body count—it gives me nightmares.

"Does he know if Tommy is still alive?"

Scarlett pulls back from me. We're about the same height, though she's slightly taller than my five-foot-four. "He's not with him, Skye. I would've told you if I knew anything, I promise."

The sincerity in her voice is not fake, and that loosens some of the emotion I'm feeling. "No more keeping things from me. You're the only person I have left that I trust, Scar."

Tears brim in her eyes. "I'm sorry."

"It doesn't matter now." My gaze shifts back to the window, as if I expect to see dark figures waiting among the shrubberies, but nothing moves, not even farther in the distance where the horses are grazing. I pull out my phone, still watching the horizon, only dragging my eyes away for a moment to pull up his contact details.

Connecting the call, I press my ear to the handset. It rings and rings endlessly, but there's no answer. I hang up and dial again. Still, there's nothing.

My fear is growing with every passing second, so I dial

Tommy on the third attempt. He picks up after the fourth ring. "Bug? You safe?"

Hearing his voice soothes my racing heart, but it also pisses me off. "Where's my father?"

"He's uh… busy."

"Too busy to pick up a call from his daughter?" I can't mask how annoyed I am and I don't try to, so I know Tommy will be cringing at my tone.

I hear a rustling sound, and the voices in the background of the call get quieter. "You call just to give me shit?" he demands after a moment.

"I'm stuck here, alone, worrying every second of the day that my phone is going to ring so I can hear that you or my dad are dead. So, yeah, Tommy, I'm giving you shit."

"Bug, this ain't about you."

"No, it's about vengeance or whatever fucking crusade you're on."

"They killed my brother. They've killed multiple men I've stood shoulder-to-shoulder with. You too. So, yeah, we're on a fucking crusade. You have no idea the lines that have been crossed to keep you safe."

Cold spreads through my spinal column before encasing my heart in an icy prison. "What lines?"

What have you done, Tommy?

I have no illusions that the Pioneers are dangerous, that my father is the most dangerous of them all, but this statement fills me with dread.

"It doesn't matter."

"It matters to me! What the hell is going on?"

He blows out a breath, making the line crackle. "You just need to sit tight and wait it out."

That response is the worst thing he could have said. It adds a spark to an already burning fire. I'm tired of being kept in the dark. I'm sick of feeling that constant dread in my stomach.

"I'm done waiting. I'm done sitting around and dreading every time my phone rings. I'm fucking done!"

"You don't get to be done. You're a Richardson."

"No, Tommy. I'm not. My father has made it perfectly clear that I am not a part of his organisation, and you know what? For the first time ever, I'm happy not to be."

"What the fuck does that mean?" His tone is unlike anything I've ever heard from him. There's a dark bite that sounds nothing like him. Once more, I realise how far my best friend has sunk into the world my father has built.

"It means I'm done. I'm just fucking done. This isn't my life. It's yours and my father's, and I'm just… here. Existing. No more. You want to get yourself killed, by all means, do it, but I'm done."

"No, you ain't done and you'll never be done. Pioneer blood flows in your veins."

"Tell my father I'll send him a message when I know where I'm going."

"Skye," he grits out my name, "you ain't going anywhere."

"And who's going to stop me? The guards? Oh, yeah, they aren't here."

He doesn't speak, which heightens my nerves. "Who

told you that?"

"I don't need to be told, Tommy. I've got eyes. I'm assuming since they're gone, I'm safe to be here alone, which means I'm safe to be anywhere alone."

"You've always been safe, Skye. You think your dad would've left you if you weren't?"

I want to believe that, but not every word out of Tommy's mouth rings true.

Lines have been crossed...

Would I be a line this motorcycle club would cross too? If that's the case, I'm safer out of this house. Everyone knows this place belongs to my father.

"If I'm safe, then there's no reason for me to stay locked in the house, is there?"

"You ain't leaving, Skye."

"If you were here, you might be able to stop me, but you're not, so I'm going to live my life while you're off doing whatever you're doing."

I can sense his rage down the line, but even so, the vitriol he spews shocks me.

"Why are you being such a fucking bitch about this?"

I gasp, stunned into momentary silence before I find my voice again. "If I'm being such a bitch, then why do you care what I'm doing?"

"I don't have time for whatever fucking tantrum this is. Do whatever you want, Skye, but you're the one who will have to face your dad."

Before I can form a reply, the line goes dead. I pull the phone away from my ear and stare at the screen. Bastard.

Tears burn my eyes, and not because I'm upset but

because I'm furious. I want to call him back and scream at him, but I know he won't answer now. For all that he called my outburst a tantrum, he's pretty good at throwing them himself.

Why am I expected to put my life on hold while they play out their war? My father doesn't respect me enough to tell me what's going on, and Tommy thinks I'm a spoiled bitch for wanting more. How does that make me spoiled?

"Are you all right?" Scarlett asks, speaking slowly as if she expects me to erupt, but my anger is not for her, and I won't unleash it on her either.

"No, Scar, I'm not." The tightness in my throat feels like it's choking me.

"You serious about leaving?"

"Yep," I reply, popping the 'P'. "I want to leave this fucking house. I'm sick of looking at these four walls. I'm sick of sitting around like a good little princess waiting for news about people who clearly do not care about me."

Her mouth tugs into a smile. "I like this rebellious side of you. It's feisty."

"It's not rebellion," I mutter. "It's just time for me to grow up. If I don't leave now, Scar, I'm scared I'll never do it."

"Where are you going to go?"

"A hotel for now. Then I'm going to find an apartment in the city."

I'll have to use my dad's money to do it, but he owes me this, so I don't feel any hint of guilt about it.

"Your dad will lose his shit when Tommy tells him."

"I don't care. The longer I'm here, the more I feel like I'm suffocating." My breath is tearing out of me, my chest tight so I can't draw more air into my lungs. "I need to leave. I need to be free."

She comes to me, her hands cupping my face. Her expression is more serious than I've ever seen. "Then we'll leave. I have money in savings. We can rent a flat in the city centre together."

"You're coming with me?"

"Hell yeah, I'm coming with you. I'm not going back to my parents' place while you're living it up in the city. Just think of all the drinking and fun we can have. Tommy'll hate it, which makes it the best kind of revenge."

"This isn't about getting one over on him or my dad," I say.

"Of course not," she agrees in a tone that suggests she doesn't believe me, "but let's just pretend it is for a little while, okay?"

I grin at her. "We'd better pack and get out of here. Tommy will have told my dad, and he'll send his minions to stop me."

"Then go quickly."

I pack as much as I can fit into two suitcases, including makeup and some shoes. I also grab my passport, birth certificate, and other important documents from Dad's office. Dad calls me repeatedly as I gather all my stuff, but I don't answer. I silence my phone instead.

I don't want him to talk me out of this.

I shove my phone in my pocket and glance around my bedroom to see what else I need. I've spent my entire life in this room. It grew with me. The pony wallpaper was covered with posters of my favourite bands until it was redecorated a few years ago. The memories I have nearly overwhelm me, especially the ones of my mum.

Before she died, I remember her lying with me on my bed and listening to music while we talked. It wasn't usual, but it's my favourite memory of her.

There are a few photographs of us together on my dresser top and bedside table that I carefully pack away.

I linger on a photo of Tommy and me when we were around ten years old. His beaming smile is so carefree and easy. I wish we could go back to those days.

I grab the photograph and put it with the others I've packed then I zip everything up. Getting my luggage down the stairs is a challenge, and I'm sweaty by the time I reach the foyer.

Scarlett is already waiting for me with one suitcase. She'd packed light to stay over, but she says nothing about how much I have.

"I called a cab. It'll be here in a couple of minutes."

I nod, ignoring how breathless I feel.

I'm really doing this...

In the throes of my anger, I felt righteous, but the first tendrils of doubt are starting to creep in. What if this is a mistake? Tommy was right about one thing—my dad is definitely losing his shit right now, and ignoring his calls is only going to add to that. I don't really know what he'll do. He won't hurt me, I know that, but Desmond Richardson is not a man used to being defied, and up until this moment, I never have.

I've pushed boundaries, sure, but this is so much more than that.

"You okay?" Scarlett questions.

"Yeah, I'm good. Let's wait by the gate."

She helps me with one of my suitcases and together, we fumble our way over to the gate at the front of the property. As I'm closing it behind us, a car pulls in and I hold my breath until I see the taxi sign on the side panel.

The driver helps us get the suitcases loaded, though we have to put some stuff in the front seat. I pull my belt on as Scarlett sits next to me in the back. My heart is thundering in my chest, and I let out a shaky breath as the taxi pulls out onto the main road.

Scarlett reaches between us and grabs my hand, squeezing it so hard, my bones hurt. "Whatever happens, we're in this together."

"Together," I agree.

The drive into the city centre takes over thirty minutes, and the entire time, my phone is vibrating against my leg. I don't pull it out of my pocket. Instead, I watch out the side window. For the first time in my life, I feel free.

I'm going to miss my horses, though I know they'll be taken care of by the staff. But I can't think about that in this moment. All I can focus on is moving forwards for me.

The taxi driver drops us at a hotel close to an area Scarlett says has some good clubs and bars. It's also strategically positioned in Pioneers territory. As reckless as I'm being, I'm not so stupid to put Scarlett and myself in danger. Besides, the moment I use my credit card to pay for our room, my father will know where I am. That's unavoidable until I can start earning my own money. He probably already knows where I am.

I pay for a room for three days, and we lug our shit to the lift. Scarlett uses the key card to access the room. There's a double bed against the wall and a bank of windows that look out over the city.

Scarlett goes to the door that leads to her adjoining suite. She pokes her head through before turning back to me. "You going to be okay?"

"I want cocktails."

"Get showered and changed. I know a good bar close by."

This doesn't surprise me. Scarlett has spent a lot of time in the city. Me? I wasn't allowed to do anything.

"Okay."

She disappears into her room with her suitcase, and as soon as the door snicks shut, my adrenaline flees.

What the hell am I doing?

I pull my phone out, seeing multiple missed calls and messages. I don't read them. I don't need to. I can guess what my father will have said in them.

I send a message to him, telling him that I'm safe but I'm not staying at the house anymore waiting for him. I don't give him the address of the hotel. It'll show in a few days on my bank statement anyway and he'll know then.

For now, I plan to enjoy my newfound freedom, so the first thing I do is switch my fucking phone off.

CHAPTER 8
RAGE

The Birmingham chapter's clubhouse is located on an old industrial estate similar to London's. It's tucked behind warehouses and large units in a quiet cul-de-sac, away from the prying eyes of the general public.

As I turn off the road and through the gates, my skin prickles and my instincts flare to life. Birmingham had beef with the Pioneers long before Manchester, and while their eyes have turned north to us, that doesn't give me any peace of fucking mind.

"Keep your eyes and ears peeled while we're here," I say to Ralph, who is sitting in the passenger seat next to me, his own body tight with the same tension.

"Yeah," he mutters his agreement.

I'm barely six months older than him and was not long ago wearing the same prospect patch, but the three-piece colours on my back makes me a full brother and gives me the lead here.

Ralph is nothing like me. He's quieter than a fucking corpse but dependable. I've never seen him get into a scrap that wasn't instigated by someone else, though he's always the first one in to help. His temper is non-existent, and I don't think I've seen him lose his cool once in the time I've been with Manchester.

Like I said… he's nothing like me.

Do Howler and Blackjack look at this guy and wish I was more like him?

I need you to prove why they call you Rage.

That's what Howler said to me when I first got here. He wanted… no, he *needed* that beast that resides inside me to show up in this war. I just don't know how to do that without pissing people off.

I guide the van into a space reserved for visitors and cut the engine. I don't want to dwell on my shitty past decisions, not when we're in a situation that could be dangerous.

Ralph peers through the windscreen at the building, his eyes squinting against the brightness of the security light illuminating the shimmering row of motorcycles. The rest of the parking area is in shadow, and I take a moment to scan the darkness for any threats.

Can't be too careful with these psychos.

They'd attacked me, Hawk, and Blackjack less than a street away from the clubhouse. They'd tried to kill Trick in the middle of the day. Desmond Richardson and his band of maniacs have already shown us that they ain't too bothered about being seen or caught.

"You been here before?" I don't turn to Ralph as I ask this question, but I can sense the prospect's tension.

"Once, with Trick."

Trick... the cause of all this crap raining down on us. I don't understand the way everyone fucking protects him and yet expects me to rein in my shit. He's a looser cannon than I'll ever be.

"Have you?"

"Yeah." More times than I can count. It's the closest chapter to London, and as a prospect, I was the guy who had to do the miles, usually with another patched brother.

Ralph eyes the building without moving or letting a single emotion cross his face. Finally, he sits back in his seat. "You think there'll be trouble?"

My shoulders draw up. "I don't know what the fuck to expect," I admit, and that's what has me so on edge.

The Pioneers have territory here and farther out of the city. Their focus has been laser pinpointed on Manchester rather than here, though that could change at any time. Trick's one-man crusade puts a huge target on the back of anyone wearing a Sons kutte.

I don't know what, if anything, Crank has been doing behind the scenes to support us. That information is way above my pay grade both as a newer patch and as the newest member into Manchester. I don't like the Birmingham chapter President much. He makes the hairs on the back of my neck prickle, and I've learned to trust that shit.

Knowing we can't stay in the van forever, I open the

driver's door and climb out, trying for a confidence I don't feel. I'll never walk into a situation without wearing that shit like a cloak.

My hand strays to my hip, where my flick knife is kept, as I close the door behind me and face the building.

Coming here ain't punishment—that's what I was told, anyway—but it fucking feels like it. This is a shit job, a prospect's one. Ain't a single reason for me to be here when our chapter is a target.

Pushing that down, I try to drown out the poisonous anger beginning to swirl in my gut. It doesn't matter why I'm here, only that I am, and I have to prepare for every and all eventualities.

I take a moment to scan the parking area for danger. There's no one around, though I can hear music coming from the clubhouse itself.

The lack of security concerns me. Where the fuck is everyone?

"You thinking it's fuckin' weird the front door is just—"

"Unmanned?" Ralph finishes.

"Yeah," I say.

Something moves in the darkness at the side of the building not bathed in light. My hand moves in a flash, pulling my knife free and flicking the blade open. I'm ready to fight when a deep chuckle resonates through the air and a figure steps out of the shadows.

"You gonna stick me with that little knife, Rage?"

The hand wrapped around my heart loosens as I realise who it is.

Phoenix.

It's his real name, though he goes by Nicky. I don't think I've ever heard a brother call him anything else on the few occasions I've been in his presence.

"Fuck," I breathe out the word, "I was half a beat from killing you."

Last time I was here, he was just a regular member, but as he steps farther into the light, I see the Sergeant at Arms patch on his leather.

I don't mention his promotion as he pulls a cigarette out the inside pocket of his kutte and puts it to his lips, though I'm not surprised. Nicky is built like a fucking tank, something most SAAs have in common, with a buzz cut and arms like tree trunks. I'm a good fighter, but he could squash me like a bug without even flexing a muscle, though in one of my rages, I'd put up a good fight.

"That thing you're carrying even capable of nicking the skin?" He snorts, and then his face is illuminated by the dancing flame of his lighter as he cups his hand around it.

I don't like the smell of cigarettes. Too many fucking memories of another life. Too many burn marks on my skin from my deluded father. It takes everything I have not to step back so I don't have to breathe in his second-hand smoke and find myself stuck in a past I want to leave buried.

"Why don't I test it and find out?" I smile at him, though there's a hint of malice in it.

He laughs again. "Heard a rumour you're with Manchester now."

My spine tenses and instantly my defences go up. Where the fuck is this going? "Ain't a rumour."

He seems surprised by my answer. "Guessin' that wasn't your choice."

Not even a little, but I keep my smile in place. He outranks me, but I don't owe him an explanation. "London… Manchester… what do you care where I put my head at night?"

"I don't." He takes a long drag on his cigarette, the ember at the tip glowing red as he does. "Just makin' conversation, you miserable shite. You should try it some time."

I stare at him, a buzz of annoyance flaring through me. Is he trying to get a rise out of me? "You low on prospects?"

"No, why?"

"I walked right through the front gate unchallenged. Considering the shit going down…"

Nicky steps closer and the atmosphere suddenly becomes thick and dangerous. "You don't see me standing right here?" His words are tight, thick. "I didn't need to challenge you. I knew you were comin'. Know the reg of the van. Knew it was you."

Fuck. Me and my big fucking mouth. Ain't even got into the building and I'm already pissing someone off.

I hold my hands up in a defensive stance. "Didn't mean to offend. The shit going down has us all on edge."

He sniffs, his expression annoyed. Club safety falls to him as SAA, and I just put my fucking foot right in it. "You here to see Crank?"

I don't mistake the change of subject for forgiveness. I know better. I'm going to need to watch my mouth while I'm here.

"Yeah." I don't explain more than that. "He about?"

Nicky is a brother and he's club, but he ain't Manchester. He doesn't get to know our business.

"He's inside, probably balls deep in Chloe." I don't miss the bitterness in his words.

I try to remember anyone by that name, but nothing is clicking. "Who's Chloe?"

He takes another drag of his cigarette, blowing the smoke out in an irritated huff. "A fuckin' problem," he mutters.

I don't press, though I'm curious to know more. Not my business, not the reason I'm here either.

"Head inside. He'll be in the bar."

I glance at Ralph, and the pair of us walk over to the main doors. The music is louder as we step inside, though it doesn't sound like a party is going on—just a regular night at the clubhouse.

I trace the familiar corridor that leads into the bar area, and when I push through the door, I quickly reorientate myself. There are tables scattered around the room and a few couches pushed against one wall. Seats are filled with brothers, though not as many as I'd expect, considering the time.

I spot Crank instantly, sitting on one of the couches, a dark-haired girl about my age curled up against his side. Crank is older than her by a good twenty years, maybe more, but since she ain't fighting him, I keep my nose out of shit that doesn't concern me.

As I approach, Crank's gaze moves to me, and he watches every step I take towards him with a scrutiny that makes my fingers curl into fists. The girl glances up at me too, her fingers tracing patterns on Crank's chest.

He signals with one finger in a circular motion for me to turn around. I grit my teeth but do as he asks, showing my back before I turn to face him again.

"So, the rumours are true," he says. "You're under Howler now."

I'm not sure why everyone is so interested in my shit, but I keep that to myself. Mouthing off at Nicky is one thing, but Crank is a President. Granted, he ain't my President, but he's still someone I don't want to piss off. "That's what the patch says."

He laughs under his breath, but his eyes aren't full of mirth. The girl, who I assume is 'the problem' Nicky mentioned, peers up at me as she rests her head on Crank's shoulder. She doesn't look like a club whore, and she's obviously someone important to him, considering he ain't shoving her off. "Still a gobshite, I see. Seem to remember telling you the last time you were here that mouth of yours was an issue."

I don't want to get into it with Crank, not like this, so I change the subject. "Howler sent us." I glance at the girl, not willing to say anything else in front of her.

"Yeah. Shipment's coming in first thing. The boys'll load you up as soon as it arrives. For now, grab a drink, grab a woman, and enjoy some Birmingham hospitality.

The girls have opened room three for you, and there'll be a bunk for the prospect."

The last thing I want to do is stay here, but we're on Crank's timeline, so I force a smile. "Appreciate that."

He ignores me, his attention going back to the girl at his side. Dismissed, I wander over to the bar, Ralph at my back.

"What can I get you, sugar?" one of the club bunnies asks as she saunters over. The cropped top she's wearing barely contains her tits and the shorts are just as tiny, revealing a strip of tanned skin on her stomach.

I need alcohol, lots of it, but not here, not surrounded by club. I can feel the gazes of the men in the room coming to me, wondering why I'm wearing the Manchester rocker and not London. I don't want to explain my shit, and I know there's going to be questions. Brothers don't usually move between chapters without a reason, and I'm sure every single person in this room can guess why I did. The failure I feel at being pushed out by Ravage is a barb in my stomach.

"You know what, sweetheart? I'm gonna pass," I say, not missing the disappointment on her face.

Fresh meat is probably a commodity here, and although fucking my problems away sounds appealing, I don't want to do it with all these eyeballs on me. I turn to Ralph. "Find me in the morning. I want to blow out of here as early as we can."

"Sure. You need me, just message."

I clamp a hand on his shoulder before I head out to the van. I can't make out Nicky, but I'm sure that fucker is sitting in the shadows somewhere. I take my holdall into the clubhouse and climb the stairs to the room Crank gave me.

I can hear someone fucking in one of the rooms as I pass, trying to block out the sound of the woman's pants and moans. I'm not a prude. My club brothers like to fuck their old ladies anywhere and at any time, and I'm hardly a fucking virgin, but it rubs me wrong tonight.

I find the room I was assigned quickly and open the door, shoving inside and fumbling for the light switch. As soon as the space is illuminated, I take a moment to glance around.

It's small, with a double bed and furniture older than I am, cream walls, and thick curtains at the window. It's only for one night, and I can guarantee my digs are better than Ralph's. I've slept in that bunkroom with the other prospects. He won't get much fucking sleep.

I dump my bag at the foot of the bed and shrug out of my kutte, placing it on the bed before I sink onto the edge of the mattress.

The past few days have been something else, and glancing around this room, I can't help but think that despite what Howler said, this *is* punishment for my actions.

Fuck.

I scrub a hand over my jaw. There's no point dwelling on what's been done. I can't change it, but I don't know where this leaves me when I get back from this run.

My phone trills in the silence of the room, making me

jolt. I fish it out of my pocket and see the name on the screen. Hawk.

For a moment, I consider ignoring it, but it ain't worth the shit I'll get. Besides, something might have happened back at the clubhouse.

I swipe a finger over the screen and press the handset to my ear. "Yeah?"

"You arrived?"

"About ten minutes ago."

"Good. Ralph's driving ain't exactly safe. I was worried."

It's not. He tries to drive cages like they're bikes. "That's why he didn't drive."

There's a beat of silence. "You drove?"

"Yeah. Ain't a princess. I don't need to be chauffeured around."

"You do remember the fact you were unconscious less than twenty-four hours ago?" He sounds irritated, which pisses me off.

"And whose fault was that?"

He huffs down the line. "You gonna hold that against me forever?"

The audacity of this fucking guy… "Yeah, Hawk, I'm gonna hold it against you. You punched me the fuck out."

"I know." There's an awkward pause before he speaks again. "I shouldn't have done it."

I'm not sure if it's an apology, but I figure it's as close as I'm going to get from the man. "Did you need something?" I want to get the fuck off the phone.

"I just… be careful while you're there, okay?"

My back straightens. "Why?"

"Crank… he's… look, kid, he ain't the kind of brother to have your back."

"Meaning what?"

"I was a member of Birmingham before I came to Manchester," he admits.

"Yeah, I know that." I had been told that after meeting Hawk once when visiting one of the other chapters with Titch. I'd been a prospect back then and I didn't know what the fuck a nomad was. Titch explained, though he didn't say why Hawk had left.

"I left because of Crank. The Pioneers came at us first. They killed brothers and kids while he sat back and did nothing. All he cared about was keeping his seat and not ruffling any fucking feathers."

That should shock me, but knowing what I do about him, it doesn't. I always assumed Crank was that kind of man even before being told it. I've seen men in power, been under two different Presidents with very different leadership styles, but I trust both Howler and Rav to have the backs of every man under them. Crank… I don't get that vibe from him.

"I shouldn't be telling you this, but I can trust you, right?"

"Yeah," I agree, "you can."

I might be a hothead, but I ain't a disloyal one.

"Ravage wants Crank gone after the dust settles with all this Pioneer bullshit."

My eyes flare. *Fuck*. Removing a President ain't something that's done lightly, and it ain't something that's going to be easy. "Shit."

"Yeah, shit. Ain't sure if Crank knows it or not, but if he does, that makes him dangerous as hell. I can't see that prick giving this up without a fight, and that's gonna put the club into some kind of civil war between the chapters."

"So, even if we come out of the mess with the Pioneers, we still ain't gonna have peace."

"Depends how fast shit can be handled," Hawk says, sounding a little unsure.

"Why are you telling me this?"

"Because despite all the shit going on, you're one of us, and I don't think you had that in your head when you walked out. You ain't a prospect. You're a patched brother, and you're right, you deserve the respect that the patch brings. That means knowing this kind of thing."

I laugh. "Ain't one of you. You all think I'm a dumb kid."

"You're nineteen. We're all dickheads at that age. I sure as fuck was. Look, Ravage sees something in you, so does Howler. After what you did with those Pioneers, I see it too. You ain't the guy to sit on the sideline and watch a brother get hurt. That's a hell of an asset in this life."

I don't know if that's meant to be reassuring. "Is that meant to make me feel better?"

"No. It's just the truth. I'll be honest, you pissed me off earlier when we found Trick's handiwork. Ain't gonna deny that. I've known Trick a long time, Blackjack even longer. It was hard to hear the shit you were saying, even if you're right."

"It's harder being on the other side of it, Hawk. I get judged for every little thing I do. That guy is creeping around the city doing shit that puts a target on the whole club and he gets defended."

"Yeah, I know. It's a shit storm, and I know it seems like we're giving you a hard time while letting Trick get away with everything, but I promise you, Rage, it ain't like that. Trick's hurting. He watched his wife die in front of him. His *pregnant* wife. His daughter had to be cut out of her while she was dead. He's fucked up. Anyone would be."

I've never thought about kids or having an old lady. There's never been anyone important enough in my life to give a shit about, so I don't know how I would feel in Trick's shoes, but knowing my temper, I'd be doing far worse than he is.

"I get that. It just pisses me off when I get shit for saving your lives."

"You and he ain't on the same page, Rage. Not even close. He's gonna come back into the fold, and at that point, he's gonna have to make amends for what he's done, but first, we need to bring him home. We don't give up on family. Trick's family."

My lips curl into a snarl. "But I'm not, right?"

"You don't listen too good, do you? You're fucking family too. That's why I'm trustin' you with this shit. That's why I'm on this call trying to apologise."

That takes some of the wind out of my sails. "That was an apology?"

"Obviously not a good one, but if you need the words, I'll give them. I'm sorry, Rage. We should've handled things better, but the path you're on, it ain't a good one and we all see it. We all want to pull you off it and onto a better one."

"You want me to be someone I'm not."

The exasperated breath he lets out says more than any words. "Brother, you have to stop seeing it as you versus the world."

"Hard to do that, Hawk, when that's how it's always been," I say.

"Yeah, I get that. I had that same anger inside me when I went nomad, but that shit, it eats you up. It destroys you, Rage."

I don't tell him I've been destroyed since the day I walked out and left my father to burn. "How do you fix it?"

"You don't need to be fixed, brother. You ain't broken. Just don't let the anger consume you." He sighs. "You've got potential to be a hell of a brother and asset to this club. That anger… we want it. We need it, but at the right times. You get control of it, and you could rise right up the ranks of this club."

That isn't something I ever considered, but the thought ain't exactly unappealing. Officers get more money, better opportunities, and respect.

"I won't cause any shit while I'm here," I assure.

"Good. We got enough problems as it is. Be careful there, okay?"

"Yeah, will do."

The line goes dead, and I pocket my phone, unsure what the fuck to make of everything Hawk said. I shower and change into a clean pair of jeans and a plain white tee when I'm done. I need a drink, or ten, but there's no fucking way I can sit in the bar downstairs. Aside from facing an inquisition about my move from London to Manchester, I now have the added bonus of wondering who the hell is loyal to Crank or the rest of the club.

I'm debating grabbing a bottle from the bar and drinking in the room when there's a knock on the door.

I stare at it for a moment before I push up and open it. Nicky is leaning against the door jamb.

"You busy?"

I bite back the sarcastic remark I want to make. Hawk would be proud. "Nope."

"You want to come on a job with me?"

I want to ask more, but I don't want to seem like a paranoid bastard, especially considering the shit I know. I feign a confidence I don't feel. "Sure."

I wander over to the bed and sink onto the edge of it to pull on socks and then my boots. Once they're laced up, I grab my wallet and reach for my kutte.

"You still got that knife you pulled on me earlier?" he asks as I step out the room, closing the door behind me.

"Yeah. Expecting trouble?"

He shifts his shoulders. "Not really, but the Pioneers have a base here and they don't like us. Pays to be vigilant."

He leads me out the building, passing the bar as we make our way down the corridor. The hum of music and voices is quieter than earlier, and I wonder if Crank is still in there.

I wonder if he knows what's coming for him.

When I took the patch, Nox told me what happens if I disgrace the Sons, and none of it is good. Crank's in for a shit time, but the fucking coward should have done more.

The air is cold as we step out into the darkness. I rub my hands together to keep warm as Nicky leads me over to a car. I hate being a passenger, but I'm trying to be the bigger and better person, so I climb in while he gets into the driver's side.

The journey doesn't take long, the bright lights of the city lining the road as we make our way. He pulls up outside what looks like a bar. The sign over the door is illuminated and says 'Embers'. There's a line of people queuing along the front of the building, and I can tell by the clientele this place attracts city dwellers with money. The women are wearing dresses that probably cost more than my entire wardrobe. The men too.

"This a club-owned bar?" I peer through the windscreen to get a better look.

Nicky snorts. "Fuck no. This look like the kind of place we'd manage? The fuck who owns it is Simon Lassiter. He has six bars in the city, but this one is his biggest money spinner. We provide protection from the Pioneers and other gangs that run in the city. In return, we get a cut of the profits made."

Both London and Manchester run similar operations, so it makes sense to me that Birmingham would make money this way.

"So, we're just getting the money and leaving?"

"No. This prick is avoiding me. I'm done waiting. Given your reputation, figured you might be able to incentivise him to pay up."

This shit is where I flourish. I love delivering violence, but Hawk's fucking voice is in my head, reminding me to control myself.

As I reach for the door handle, Nicky says, "Take your kutte off."

I snap my head towards him. "What the fuck?"

Nicky shifts his shoulders. "Orders from Prez. We don't wear our colours in the city. Too much risk. Pioneers have territory close by where we're going. We've lost too many brothers to put that target on our backs."

I understand the reasoning, and part of me maybe even agrees, but I'm not hiding who I am. "Ain't takin' my kutte off, Nicky."

If Ravage knew this shit was going on, he'd lose his mind. We wear our colours proudly. We don't fucking hide behind our fear.

Before I can speak, Nicky holds up a hand. "I know what you're gonna say."

"I highly doubt that," I mutter.

"I don't like it either. Trust me, I've had more fucking arguments with Crank and Grub about this shit, but we're on the front line of a war. We've been fighting with these fucking maniacs a hell of a lot longer than you have. We've watched brothers die, old ladies fall apart, families get torn to pieces. You go out there with it on and all you're doing is making yourself a target. Pioneers, they got eyes everywhere. Ain't ready to die yet, and I ain't having Howler kick my arse if I get you killed, so take it off." When I don't move to do it, he sighs. "It's a compromise we have to make to keep doing business."

"It a shit one," I grumble, but, gritting my teeth, I shrug out of my kutte, the leather creaking as it moves. Hawk told me I needed to think more before I act, so I take in Nicky's words and reasoning. I hate taking it off, but I don't want to get a brother killed either.

Folding it, I place it under the seat, hidden from view, and get out the car. Nicky does the same and rounds the front of the vehicle. As we approach the main door, Nicky heads for the bouncers rather than the queue. The two guys on the door are huge, one with a shaved head, the other with short, dark hair and a mean-looking scar on his face. They exchange a quick glance as we approach, and I can tell instantly shit is going to get ugly.

"Ain't letting you in, Nicky," the shaved head man says.

"You thinking to stop me, Walt?" There's a lightness in his tone that's not mirrored on his face.

'Walt' swallows, and I can see the fear in his eyes as he takes in Nicky and then me. "Boss's orders."

"The boss ain't the one about to get shanked."

"Come on, Nicky, this shit ain't our fault. We're just following orders."

Nicky grabs the other man's throat and shoves him back against the wall near the open door. His eyes flare wide and terror flickers in them.

The gasp from the queue has my gaze shifting in that

direction. There's a mix of horror and excitement on the faces of the customers waiting to gain entry. People love to watch violence, no matter how much they deny it.

"You're gonna get me fired," Walt complains.

"Fired is better than dead," I say.

Nicky releases his throat and pats his cheek before gesturing for me to follow him inside.

The corridor is barely lit, the black walls making it feel oppressive. Music thumps through the floor beneath my boots as we get closer to the end of it and I wait while Nicky opens the door, a blast of bass assaulting my ears.

He steps through the door, and I follow behind him, my eyes adjusting to the darkened room. There are booths lining the room, groups of people sitting in them, illuminated by the soft orange glow of a light in the centre of each table. The bar runs the length of the back wall, and there are workers in crisp white dress shirts with dark waistcoats overtop rushing around with cocktail shakers and bottles that I'm sure are fucking expensive. Towards the back of the room, there is a small dance floor that's empty except for two lone women swaying around their tall, stemmed glasses.

Nicky wanders over to the bar, and I follow, waiting while he asks one of the staff to find Simon Lassiter. I turn back to the room, scanning for threats, and that's when I see her.

She's sitting in a booth with a blonde girl opposite her, talking animatedly. On the surface, the blonde is model beautiful, but it's the other woman my eyes are magnetised to. Her soft brown hair is curled in those loose waves a lot of the old ladies seem to wear these days, and her pert little tits are pushed up in her dress, making perfect globes. It's fucking sexy as hell.

I'm drawn to that perfect nose, sculpted dark brows, and her full mouth that begs to be kissed. She ducks her head as she rolls the stem of her glass between her fingers, smiling.

I don't know what triggers her awareness that she's being watched, but her eyes lift to scan the room, a dip appearing between her brows as she tries to find the source of her prickling senses.

Adrenaline floods my system as I wait for her to find me, and it seems to take an eternity for her eyes to lock to mine.

As soon as she and I are connected, my heart thuds savagely beneath my sternum and my need to go to her almost has my feet moving.

I can't read the look she's giving me, but she hasn't looked away yet, and I don't know what the fuck to make of it.

"Rage?" Nicky's voice has me snapping my head back to him. He's standing in the doorway, ready to go inside. "You coming?"

"Yeah," I say, following him inside, but my eyes slide back to the girl in the booth one more time before we step through a door that says 'Staff Only'.

CHAPTER 9
SKYE

"Earth to Skye." Scarlett waves her hand in front of my face, forcing my eyes to tear away from the man at the bar.

"Sorry," I murmur, resisting the urge to turn back towards him.

It's a powerful desire swirling inside me, more potent than anything I've ever felt. My heart is thumping a hundred miles per hour in my chest, and my skin feels too hot, even though the dress I'm wearing isn't covering much of my body.

Scarlett grasps her glass and places the thin straw between her pursed lips as she takes a sip. "These cocktails are amazing."

I smile, agreeing with her before I risk glancing back in the direction of my mysterious voyeur. He's no longer standing at the bar, and a strange disappointment rushes through me.

"Do you think your dad knows where we are yet?" Scarlett asks.

I glance around as if expecting one of his men to jump out from behind a booth, but all I see is people having a good time. "He'll find us eventually," I say.

I'm not naive enough to believe this plan has any longevity, but even just this taste of freedom is dizzying. I've never been anywhere before without guards, or Tommy, on my heels. I feel like a normal eighteen-year-old girl on a night out with my friend, and I never want to give this up.

Tonight, I'm not Skye Richardson.

I'm just... *me*.

I take a long sip of my glass, the strength of the alcohol hidden beneath the fruity flavours of the cocktail. I like the way my head feels light, my shoulders too. My worries and fears are drifting off as the buzz in my body grows.

"You think he'll come himself or send Tommy?"

I don't think this is the kind of disobedience my father will leave someone else to handle.

"Tommy's just as likely to strangle me as my father. He's not a better alternative. Anyway, I don't want to talk about them. I want to drink until I can't feel my toes."

"And maybe get laid?" I scoff at her. The last thing on my mind right now is sex. Scarlett rolls her eyes. "I know Tommy is the only guy in your life, babe, but waiting for him to show up is kind of pointless. He's a Pioneer. Your dad owns him now."

Has she lost her mind? "You think I'm sitting around waiting for Tommy to come home?"

She laughs as if I've told the funniest joke. "Everyone thinks that. I know you've fucked him. I'm not blind to how he is with you. Tommy loves you, and you love him. No one thinks that relationship is platonic, Skye."

What the fuck?

Grabbing my drink, I put the straw between my lips and take a huge sip while trying to control the anger burning inside me. When I'm done, I place the glass back on the table. "Are you drunk? Is that what this is? There's nothing between Tommy and me. Not like that anyway. I won't deny that I love him, and I'll always love him, but I don't want to be with him. I never have."

The disbelieving glare Scarlett gives me makes my stomach clench.

"Yeah, right," she scoffs, "'cause when he's looking at you, he's really thinking that you're his sister. He panders to you as if you are everything to him. *Skye-bug, what do you need? Skye-bug, let me get you that.* You're telling me you've *never* fucked him, and he still does all that for you?"

What the hell...

My cheeks heat, though not from embarrassment. I'm *pissed*. "Tommy's not into me, Scarlett, and I've never *fucked him.*" I lean forwards over the table to hiss the last part, despite the fact it's loud in here and I doubt anyone can hear us.

She sits back against the velvet of the booth's back. "I know you're not a virgin, so if you didn't lose it to Tommy, then who?"

I try to keep my face neutral. My first time hadn't been

flowers and rainbows, and it definitely hadn't been with fucking Tommy.

"I didn't realise my sex life was so important to you."

Scarlett shifts her shoulders. "It's not, but I don't understand why you're hiding who was your first if it wasn't Tommy. We don't have secrets, Skye. When you told me you'd had sex for the first time, you made me believe it was with Tommy."

"I didn't say it was him." I hadn't. I'd been careful not to say anything and let her draw her own conclusions.

Jack dropped me off at home after a party one night. I don't even remember what happened, but one moment we were talking in the kitchen, and the next, Jack's tongue was in my mouth. His kisses were bruising and dominant. He was so different from his brother, and I craved him.

I was drunk when he took me upstairs, giddy on kisses and the alcohol I'd consumed. When he laid me down on the bed and hoisted my dress up over my thighs, I let it happen. I wanted it. I wanted to know why Scarlett thought this was such a big deal.

Jack looked in my eyes as he pressed the tip of his cock against my centre, and I saw the emptiness in his gaze. He was eighteen, a Pioneer already, and I thought I wanted this.

I didn't expect it to hurt as much as it did, but I was so tight, and he seemed impossibly big. I couldn't move as he rutted against me, driving deeper with each thrust. I clung to the bedsheets, trying not to cry.

It was over quickly, though it felt like he was seated inside me for an eternity. He removed the condom, did up his pants, and glanced down at me spread on the bed. "You gonna tell Tommy?" he'd asked.

Shame had crawled through me like I'd never experienced. I didn't want anyone to know what had happened in the bedroom where I played with dolls just a few short years earlier. "No."

He stared at me for a beat, his eyes dropping to between my thighs before he left. We never spoke of it again, and truthfully, I tried to pretend it never happened.

"So, if you've never been with Tommy... who was it?" Scarlett asks, bringing me back to the present.

I sit a little straighter. "No one."

"Are you still a virgin? Did you lie?"

I want to reach across the table and wrap my fingers around her skinny neck. "No."

"Then who was it?" She gives me a hurt look. "You're my best friend. We tell each other everything, Skye."

Maybe it's the alcohol, or maybe I'm just sick of keeping this secret any longer, but my mouth moves before my brain considers the consequences. "It was Jack."

Scarlett stares at me in disbelief. "Jack? Tommy's brother?" I wait for the chastisement, but it doesn't come. Instead, her lips pull into a smirk. "Your first time was with Jack?"

"I don't want to talk about this."

"Fine. You might not want to get laid, but I do. Have fun sitting on your own."

She storms off, disappearing into the crowd of people

on the dance floor. I stare after her before muttering "fucking bitch" under my breath.

No longer in the mood to drink or party, I pull out my phone, intending to book a cab, but I feel that familiar itch that tells me I'm being watched again.

I lift my head and see the man from earlier leaning against the bar, his gaze locked on me once more. I should look away, but since he's staring at me, I take my time studying him.

He's around my age, but the way he carries himself makes him seem older, like he's seen and done too much. It reminds me of the way Jack used to look—and now Tommy.

His dark hair is long enough to drip across his face to his chin, and there's ink on his neck that disappears beneath his clothes. He has a beard that's short but somehow seems as wild as his hair. Everything about him seems that way, like he's barely hanging on to his control.

Despite Ember's dress code, he's wearing a thin, long-sleeved white tee with a pair of faded light blue jeans and heavy brown boots. A chain spans from the front of his jeans to the back pocket, draped around where his hip bone would be. He looks out of place among the sharply dressed suits and tight little dresses, but the way he's standing is like he belongs in that space.

He breaks contact with me as a bigger man with a buzz cut and arms like tree trunks steps up to him. I can't hear their conversation over the music and din of voices, but I don't need to. I don't need to be any kind of expert to read their body language. The bigger guy seems irritated, but the other guy doesn't appear to care. Eventually, buzz cut throws his hands up in front of him and walks away.

The younger guy turns to face the bar, lifting a hand to signal over the bartender before glancing back over his shoulder at me.

Why the fuck is he staring at me?

Who is he?

Alcohol really does rot the brain because the only thing I can think is that he's one of my father's soldiers, sent to watch over me like I'm a fucking child.

I slip out the booth, grabbing my cocktail and sloshing it over my hand. I don't pay that any attention as I stumble over to him. He watches me through slightly narrowed eyes, but with no fear.

"Why are you watching me?" I demand as I crowd his space.

It's a mistake, but I realise it too late as he slips the bottle onto the bar and somehow steals the last inch between us. My heart thuds as a little harmless staring contest suddenly becomes a dangerous game.

What if he's not one of my father's men, but someone who wants to harm me?

I swallow down my fear, trying not to back away. The buzz in my body makes me bolder than I have any right to be. I risk taking my eyes off him for a moment to scan the dance floor for Scarlett, but I don't see her anywhere. The sea of bodies shields her from my view, causing a jolt of panic to cut through my drunkenness.

"Why does anyone watch someone else? I find you

interesting." His accent gives away his London roots, and it's deep in a way that makes my stomach flip.

I stare at him. "You find a woman you've never spoken to and only seen from across a room interesting?"

"Are you not interesting?"

My mouth opens then closes. "I'm... interesting. I'm just not interested in *you*."

He straightens, and I realise how tall he is. He looms over me, forcing my eyes to rise to meet his. "The way you were staring back says otherwise."

"I was only staring because you were looking at me."

"I thought I was argumentative, but fuck me, you're even worse."

I narrow my eyes at him, or at least I try. I'm pretty sure I'm squinting. "What does that mean?"

He shakes his head. "Doesn't matter. Where'd your friend go?"

"She's coming back," I say quickly, snapping my gaze back to him. "I'm not alone here, so don't try anything."

"And what do you think I'm going to try?"

I narrow my gaze at him. "Do you always talk in questions?"

"Sometimes."

"Are you some kind of creep?"

His brow arches in a way that I find more attractive than I should. "Do I look like a creep to you?"

He really doesn't, and I have to resist the urge to let my eyes roam over him and all his contoured muscles.

"Just answer the question."

He leans into me, and my heart stops as his warm

breath tickles along the side of my ear. Is it possible to combust from someone I just met? "Because you're fucking gorgeous and I'm not a polite person."

Shit. I pull back, forcing him to do the same. My heart is hammering a staccato beat in my chest. "What kind of person are you?"

"A dangerous one."

From anyone else, I would find that hilarious, but when he says it, I truly believe him. He oozes trouble in the same way the men in my father's organisation do. He has that storm inside him that all those lost souls who fall onto dark paths have.

"Am I supposed to be scared of you?"

"Don't like my women scared, sweetheart," he says. "I like them willing." My pussy throbs at his words. *Oh, fuck.* "You want a drink?"

I glance down at the almost empty cocktail I'm clutching like a life raft in turbulent waters. Alcohol is probably not a smart move. I'm already pretty buzzed and making crazy decisions. More booze is not going to help that.

But Scarlett's words are still a fresh wound, and I need to feel something for just one fucking night. The way he's looking at me tells me he wants to make that happen.

This kind of crazy recklessness isn't me, but I tried being a good girl. I've had moments of madness over the years—like sleeping with Jack—but right now, I feel like being wild and free.

I'm eighteen.

Girls my age pick up guys in bars all the time.

I'm just a girl in a bar, standing with a hot as hell guy who is looking at me like he wants to give me the best night of my life, and honestly, I want to let him.

Fuck Scarlett.

Fuck Tommy too.

I'm not theirs to keep under lock and key.

"Yeah, you know what? I'd love a drink."

I slide the glass onto the bar as he turns to order for me. While he does, I stare at his profile, taking in the sharp jaw line beneath that scruffy beard and my mind wanders, wondering who the hell this guy is and if there are more like him.

"What's your name?" I ask.

He casts a glance in my direction. "Do you really want to know?"

"Well, yeah… I'd like know who I'm thanking for buying me a drink."

He snorts. "Trust me, darlin', having my name won't make any difference to how this night is gonna play out."

The way he says this makes heat flood my body, settling between my legs. It drips with promise and need. "And how's that?"

He turns towards me and brushes my hair back from my face. His hands are rough, hands that are used to working. I'm pretty sure my breath is lodged in my chest as solid as a cork. "With my cock buried in your sweet cunt."

No one has ever spoken to me like that before. My father would have flayed the flesh off any man who dared. The thrill that races through me hearing his dirty words makes me think for the briefest of seconds I've lost my mind. This shouldn't be attractive, and yet my pussy clenches with need.

I've never flirted in my life, but I try because I feel like he'd like that. "I hate to disappoint, but I don't put out that easy."

Is my voice wobbly? Is my face on fire?

He reaches out and cups the side of my neck in a move so possessive, it makes my knees weak.

When did I become this girl who's taken in by a pretty face?

When he grins at me, I know I've lost this game, because there is nothing that's going to stop me from falling into this man's bed.

He dips his head to meet my gaze, his eyes granite-hard as he takes me in. "Oh, sweetheart, trust me when I tell you, nothing about tonight is gonna be easy."

CHAPTER 10
RAGE

Her cheeks flush a pretty pink at my words. I know I'm pushing her out of her comfort zone, but the way she reacts makes it fucking worth it.

I watch as she tries to find a response to me and fails. That makes me snigger. Fuck, this woman is perfect in every damn way. She's not only gorgeous but a little sassy, and I like that. Too many club bunnies say what they think you want them to. There's no independent thought.

I feel like this girl matches my energy and I've never experienced that before.

"You're kind of presumptuous," she says, taking the fresh cocktail glass I hand her and placing the straw between her pert lips.

I can't tear my eyes away as she sucks on it. I want her mouth around my cock like that.

"It's not presumptuous if it's gonna happen."

She peers up at me through those dark lashes and, fuck, I want to bend her over the bar and push inside her right now. "So, make it happen."

I take the glass from her, sliding it back on the bar, and grab her hand. She feels soft and delicate against my palm. Too good for me, but I'm not giving her up now that I've started this.

The moment I laid eyes on her sitting across the room, I wanted her. I don't know how to explain it. I've been attracted to women before, even wanted to fuck strangers I thought were hot, but with this girl… it's deeper than that. There is a carnal need for me to have her. I knew I couldn't leave the bar without tasting her, something that pissed Nicky off, but the brother will get over it.

Leading her through the crowd of people, I make for the 'Staff Only' door that Nicky and I went through before. Lassiter had been an easy problem to sort. I got to unleash a little violence, but he paid up what he owed to Nicky.

But releasing that storm inside me is always a dangerous thing. I came out of that room with sore knuckles and adrenaline blasting through my system.

I don't know if she truly knows what she's getting herself into with me. Rage by name, Rage by nature—I'm no more calm in the bedroom than I am out of it. She's an angel sent to tame a demon, and I don't know that I can hold back with her.

I shove the door open and step into the corridor behind it, still gripping her hand. There are numerous stock cupboards and a staff room in this part of the building, but it's Lassiter's office I head for.

"Where are we going?" Her voice is like silk, sliding through my brain, but I hear the slight tremble of fear in her tone. She should be afraid, but not for the reasons she's probably thinking.

"Somewhere private," I assure her, rubbing my thumb over the back of her hand.

I don't knock on Lassiter's door. I shove it open and find Simon sitting at this desk, a towel held to his bloody face. His eyes widen as he takes me in, and fuck if I don't get satisfaction from seeing his terror.

I shouldn't. I was a victim of that same thing once. My father created an atmosphere of such horror that I was scared for a long time. Reclaiming that fear and morphing it into something else is the only way I can survive.

"Out," I order.

The confusion that crosses his face would be funny, except I'm not in the mood for any shit.

"This is my office."

I don't say a word. I don't need to. The look on my face clearly conveys what will happen if he doesn't do as I ask. He scrabbles up, grabbing his suit jacket from the back of the chair.

"Fuck you," he snarls as he walks past me.

I snort at his outburst and wait for the door to shut before I round on her. She lets out a squeal as I pin her against the wall behind us. Her chest heaves, the globes of her tits begging to be touched, but I'm in no rush. I want to savour every moment of this.

"You're not good at making friends, are you?" There's humour in her words but also a hint of seriousness.

"I don't give a fuck about friends," I tell her, dipping my head and pressing my lips against her throat.

Her pulse flutters wildly against my lips as I kiss every inch of skin there, and I hear her breath tearing out of her between the small moans she's making.

"Oh," she gasps as I hit what must be a sensitive spot, "that feels good."

I don't think about her enjoyment. My only focus is on the irritation working through me. The shit back at my clubhouse, being sent to Birmingham on this stupid errand that could've been done by Ralph alone, fucking Lassiter being a dick, and Nicky giving me shit about staying. It swirls through me, and the only way I'm going to quiet the anger building again inside me is through the release sex gives me.

My left hand slides the top of her dress down enough to free one breast. She's not wearing a bra, and I can tell she's aroused by how hard her nipple is beneath the pads of my fingers. I roll it, tugging it hard enough to make her moan as I keep up my assault on her neck.

The way she's writhing around makes my cock solid in my jeans. I can't wait to get inside her. I hope the fantasy I've built in my head matches the reality.

I pull her dress down on the side, freeing her other breast, and dip to take a nipple in my mouth. Her fingers slide into my hair as I suck and circle my tongue around the left and then the right.

"Oh, fuck." She breathes the word, as if speaking it in prayer.

If she's looking for a saviour, she ain't going to find that here. I'm not a good man. I'm not even a good club brother, though I want to be.

She grabs my hand, directing me between her legs. I feel lace against my palm and wetness seeping through the material. "You're fucking soaked," I murmur in her ear. "Dirty girl."

Her eyes are challenging as she reaches between our bodies to cup my cock through my jeans. "You're not exactly unaffected either."

I smirk, stroking my fingers back and forth over her underwear as she rubs me. "I've got eyes, sweetheart. You're fucking stunning. Any man would be affected."

The coy smile she gives makes me want to tell her these things on repeat. This girl is everything.

I keep one hand stroking between her legs and curl the other around her throat. "This ain't gonna be a fairy tale encounter," I warn.

The way her tongue darts out to wet her lips almost has me coming in my jeans. Fuck, she's a dream, and I don't think it's even intentional.

"Do I look like I believe in fairy tales?"

Truthfully, she does, and that's what's going to make this all the worse. I'm a piece of shit for this, but I'm not walking away. Gripping her throat, I turn her around, so she's facing the wall, and her hands splay in front of her as she glances over her shoulder at me. There's a flash of nervousness that she quickly hides as I shove her dress up over her bottom and get my first look at the lace covering her cunt. It's pretty, black… and it's coming off. I slip the material down her legs just enough to widen her stance. She tries to step out of them, but they end up stuck around one of her ankles, the heels she's wearing making it hard for her to free herself.

My self-control is gone. All I can think about is fucking her pussy until I find my release. I grip her hips, forcing her feet back from the wall, and pressing her back down so she's bent over.

She looks good enough to eat.

My fingers skim over her lower back and her perfect arse cheeks before I pull a condom out of my wallet. I keep my eyes locked on this perfect scene of her bent over, waiting to take me as I shove my jeans down my thighs just enough to free my cock.

Her breath quickens as I tear open the condom wrapper and roll the rubber down my shaft. Her thighs rub together as she tries to relieve some of the friction she must be feeling.

I don't make her wait. I take my cock in my hand and pull the shaft twice, priming myself before I press the hard tip against her core.

With one hand on myself, the other I wrap around her hair, tugging her head back as I shove inside her. The sound she makes is fucking beautiful.

It's somewhere between a gasp and a cry. I bury myself inside her, pushing as deep as I can go until my pelvis sits flush against her arse.

I tug her head farther back, extending her neck even

more as I draw back and slam into her. She moans as I set a punishing pace, circling my hips to drive deeper inside.

Everything that was swimming through my brain starts to dissipate with every thrust into her tight channel until all I'm focused on is my heavy breaths and her whimpers.

My cock is painfully hard inside her as I drag back and forth, my grip on her hair probably uncomfortable for her, though she says nothing. She just takes everything I give her.

Her pants get more frantic, and the sounds she's making as I hammer her make me even harder. She's sagged against the wall as if it's the only thing keeping her upright, that and the grip I have on her hair as I plough deeper and harder.

"Oh, fuck," she breathes out as I slam once, twice, and then squeeze my eyes shut as my release jolts through me.

I spill into the condom as her pussy contracts around my shaft, milking more from me. My legs are weak and shaky as I slow my strokes before leaning a hand against the wall to stop from collapsing on top of her.

Sweat beads on my skin, my shirt clinging to the moisture as I try to catch my breath. Fuck. Everything feels alive as I slowly pull out of her.

My mouth is dry, my head swimming, and I have to grip the edge of the desk as I roll the condom off. At the edge of the rubber, I notice cum leaking through a small tear.

Fuck.

"You on the pill?" I knot the rubber and toss it in the bin at the side of the desk.

She doesn't answer, so I twist to look at her. She's still in the same position, her fingers splayed on the wall.

"Did you hear me?"

"Uh… no." She straightens slowly, tugging her dress over her bottom as she does. "You wrapped though. I saw you put it on."

"Did I hurt you?"

Finally, she gives me her eyes, turning to face me. "What? No. That was… short, but it was fine."

I frown at her choice of words. "Were you expecting an hour-long fuck fest?"

She laughs, but there's embarrassment in the gesture as she tucks her breasts away. Fuck, I wish she wouldn't. Those dark nipples beg to be sucked.

"I can't believe I just fucked a stranger in the back room of a bar." Her eyes squeeze shut.

"This your first one-night stand?"

"Again with the assuming." I make a grunting sound. "Well, we don't have to be strangers. I'm Skye."

I stare at her outstretched hand but don't take it. "I just had my dick in your cunt. I think it's a little late for names."

"Probably, but at least I can tell myself I'm not a total disgrace if I know your name."

I do up my jeans, fixing myself so I can go back out into the main room. "Trust me, sweetheart, having my name ain't gonna make you feel better about what we did here."

"Why won't you just say it?" She—Skye—sounds pissed, so I glance up at her. Her arms are folded over her chest, pushing her tits up in her dress, and for a moment, I debate going in for round two, but that's a stupid idea, considering how crazy she's being right now.

"You don't want to know who I am," I warn her. "Believe me, it's better you don't know."

"What does that mean?"

"Exactly that, Skye."

A deep dip appears between her eyes. "Maybe you don't want to know who I am."

I laugh. I can't help it. This angelic-looking girl ain't fooling me with that shit. "Sure." I pass her, heading to the door. "Oh, and you might want to get the morning after pill. Condom broke."

Her mouth drops open, but I'm through the door and into the main bar area before she can say a word. I thread through the people gathered around the room until I reach the front entrance.

The air outside is freezing, and I pull my phone out, intending to call Ralph for a ride, when I spot the car still parked up.

My lips tug into a smirk when I realise Nicky fucking waited for me. I wander over to where he's parked up and open the passenger side door. "Thought you were pissed at me."

He rolls his eyes. "I am fucking pissed but wasn't any way in hell I could leave you here, dickhead. What if you accidentally wandered into Pioneers territory? Howler would kill me if I got you murdered."

"Nice to know you care." I take my kutte from his outstretched hand and shrug it on, settling it back into place.

It feels so good to have it back on, and it makes me realise how much I want to stay part of this club. The Sons are in my blood now, and I've gotta do better if I'm going to keep my place.

"I don't care about you getting dead," he mutters. "I care about what happens to me if I let that happen. Get the fuck in. I want to go to bed."

Shaking my head and laughing, I climb into the car. I feel relaxed now, sated. It's amazing what a good release can do for all that tension in my body.

As I reach to pull on my seatbelt, my eyes lock onto Skye standing outside the bar. Her brows are drawn together and there's pain in her face that I don't understand until I realise she probably saw my kutte before I got in the car.

There are women who will fuck a biker just for the fun it. Some want to get that coveted place on the saddle of a brother's motorcycle. Some are desperate to be old ladies.

But Skye looks horrified that the man she just let inside her body is a biker. There's nothing good in her expression.

All those feelings of worthlessness that shrouded me for years before I found the club wash over me, and I don't like how it feels.

The calm I felt starts to morph back into anger as her hands cover her mouth while she rapidly blinks as if what she's seeing isn't real.

Fucking stuck-up, nasty bitch.

I flip her the bird as Nicky starts up the car and pulls out of the space and onto the main road. No more fucking women outside the club.

Ever.

CHAPTER 11
SKYE

I can't move, and I can't breathe either. He's standing across the street from Embers in front of a dark coloured car, but that's not what my eyes are drawn to.

It's the leather vest moulded to his back like he's been wearing it for years. The skull wearing a crown with wings coming out of it mocks me, but it's the 'Untamed Sons' arcing over the back that turns my blood to ice.

He's a biker, and he's not just any biker, he's part of the club that killed Jack—and is trying to kill my dad and Tommy.

Oh, *fuck!*

My pulse pounds frantically in my neck and chest until it's all I'm aware of. Cold spreads through my body until my teeth feel like they want to chatter together.

I screwed the *enemy*.

I had sex with a man who would've killed me, maybe

done worse, if he'd known who I am. The 'Manchester' patch wrapped around the insignia does nothing to calm my frayed nerves. He's not from Birmingham, but he's still one of them. He hates my family.

I should go back inside, find somewhere to hide until he's gone, but I'm rooted to the ground as he gets into the car. When he moves to grab his seatbelt, his gaze lifts and locks to mine.

My lungs stutter and my mouth dries.

If he knew I was Skye Richardson, I'd be dead or kidnapped—or worse. Rape is something every woman has to live in fear of, but for me, the potential of it happening is higher. There are men who would destroy me just to get to my father.

Run, Skye.

Run.

Every bone in my body feels like liquid as I try not to collapse under the weight of his stare. There have been numerous moments in the past where I've felt the icy claw of fear wrap around my heart, but I've never felt terror like this.

The engine starts, and he doesn't get out. His brows draw together as he stares at me before a flash of anger ripples over his face.

Has he figured it out?

He shakes his head before he flips me his middle finger.

I don't know what the hell that means, but he doesn't get out and come to me. He doesn't do anything but glare at me through the side window as the car pulls away from the kerb and joins traffic.

Only once the rear lights disappear around the corner do I let my shoulders sag. I want to drop to my knees and let this bottled-up emotion free, but all I do is close my eyes and take steadying breaths.

I'm safe.

I'm alive.

Fuck...

I danced with the devil and I survived. That could have gone so differently. I could be trussed up in the back of his car, waiting to be ransomed back to my father.

For the first time in my life, I understand fully the consequences of my actions. It strips away all that naivety and innocence I had, replacing it with something dark and ugly.

Reality.

I can pretend I'm normal as much as I like, but the fact is my name is a risk to my life.

"Skye?"

Scarlett's voice barely penetrates through the terror churning my gut. She's the last person I want to talk to right now.

"Go away," I whisper on a ragged breath. I'm not ready to speak to her yet. I don't even want to look at her.

Her hand on my arm has me jolting out of my skin and recoiling back from her. Scarlett blinks at me, as if stunned by my reaction.

"Are you okay?"

I want to laugh in her face. Is that a fucking joke? No,

I'm not okay. I'm not even close to being that. I can't tell if the concern she's directing at me is genuine. I see her now, a wolf in sheep's clothing, and that gores me.

"I don't want to talk to you."

I walk away from her, needing space and a moment to think about my next move.

First problem—other than the fact I screwed a man who hates my family—is the broken condom. I'm naive in a lot of ways, but I know how sex works. I know this is a bad situation if I don't take care of it.

Fucking the enemy is one thing. Having his baby is something I don't think I would be able to come back from.

My father will murder me... after he murders the biker for touching me.

The colliding panic in my mind is dizzying. I don't know what order to do anything in. I need the morning after pill. I need to get my phone and some money, both of which are at the hotel since Scarlett was supposed to be taking care of us both tonight.

Maybe there's an all-night pharmacy close to the hotel.

Is that even a thing?

I try to block out the growing soreness between my legs. He'd filled an ache inside me, even though things had happened quickly. The way he'd fucked me made me feel like I was nothing, and part of me liked it.

I don't know what that says about me. *Am I broken inside?*

Who wants to be used and discarded like that? *Someone who is starting to realise no one can be trusted.*

My hands splay over my flat belly, my gut twisting as a wave of dizziness sweeps over me. I can fix this. I just have to make a plan. Condoms break. There are solutions to that problem.

"Skye! Are you listening? I'm trying to apologise to you!" Scarlett sounds ticked off.

My fingers curl into fists at my side as I try to calm my breathing. I've never been a violent person, ironic considering the people around me, but I'm wondering if I could get away with pushing her in front of moving traffic.

"I'm listening, Scar, I just don't care what you're saying."

"I was a bitch, but I didn't mean it. Will you look at me, please?" She grabs my arm, making me wobble on my heels, and instinctively, I shove her away from me with enough force that she goes back on a foot.

"Get off me," I hiss, ignoring the shocked look she gives me. I don't care how she feels. I'm hurt and pissed at her.

"Are you going to hold this against me?" She rolls her eyes at me, as if I'm just some dumb brat. "I said some stupid things, but so did you. You weren't exactly nice either, Skye." Her voice is raw as she blurts these words, but I don't buy it—not anymore. She must see that in my face because she presses her hands together in a pleading motion. "Please, Skye, don't push me away. I love you. You're the only person I have in this world. Fuck Tommy and my brother. Fuck all of them. You and me, girl—we're all that matters."

I feel as if I'm suffocating. I rub my sternum, trying to

dislodge the trapped air beneath it. These mind games she's playing are designed to unsettle me, and they would normally, but for the first time in my life, I have clarity. This is a game to Scarlett, and I'm a pawn she's moving around her board.

"Tommy and I have never been a thing, and if you actually knew anything about me, you'd know that. If you want him, you're welcome to him."

She blows out a dry laugh, her mouth pulling into a snarl of disdain. "He's in love with *you*, Skye. That's never going to change. I see that now. Nothing I say will ever get me what I want."

"You can't make Tommy love you, Scarlett."

"He doesn't even notice me because of you." She steps into my space, trying to intimidate me, but I don't cower. I don't feel drunk any longer, My body shakes, not with fear but rage. "But he'll notice me now."

Her words are smug as she glares at me.

"What did you do, Scarlett?"

The smile that tugs at her lips is cold and unlike anything I've ever seen from her. Scarlett has been my friend for years. She stayed with me for weeks, keeping me company and soothing my fears over my father and Tommy.

Was it all a lie?

She's peeling back the layers of her deceit, and I'm held in the clutches of her darkness.

"What did you do?" I repeat, my voice an octave higher than usual.

"You'll find out."

I back away, one step, then two. Every instinct in my body tells me to run. Tears burn my eyes, and I will them not to fall. I'm not a weak girl, and I won't let her see that she has shattered me tonight.

I slip out of my heels, my gaze still locked on her, before I turn and flee. The pavement is cold under my soles, which slap against the concrete as I power my legs. I don't know what she's done, but I'm not sticking around to find out.

Adrenaline pumps through my veins, giving me the strength and speed to move quickly. I don't make it to the end of the street before I hear the squeal of brakes behind me. A large SUV-type car skids to a halt at the side of the road next to me.

Blind terror clutches me as the doors open seemingly in tandem and men in black spill out towards me.

I don't think. I just run. Behind me, I hear them giving chase, their heavy footfalls loud and gaining ground.

But I don't stop.

I'm fuelled by a will to survive. I don't know who these men are, but I know Scarlett brought them here. I approach a busy road, cars whizzing along at speed. I can't stop or I'll get caught, so I rush headlong into the traffic.

A horn blasts as a car skids to stop an inch from my legs. I feel the air move around me, but I keep running. I have no destination in mind. I don't really know where I am, but I don't stop until a SUV stops in front of me, blocking my path.

I slam into the bonnet, unable to stop in time, and

before I can push up off it, hands are on me. I scream, thrashing and fighting like a wild cat as I'm pinned to the front of the car with embarrassing ease.

The heat of the engine burns through the metal, but I'm only kept there long enough for my hands to be pulled and tied behind my back.

All thoughts empty from my mind except for two:

Who has me, and am I going to be raped?

I try to take steadying breaths as fear gallops through my stomach. The hands on me are firm, but they don't wander or touch me anywhere they shouldn't. I take a little comfort from that, but not enough to calm the thumping of my heart to a more sedate pace.

I'm pulled up off the bonnet, a hard body at my back leaving no illusion that I might be able to escape. There are two other men close by.

I narrow my eyes on them. One of them seems familiar, but I don't know. Nothing about this encounter has been friendly. The fight within me is dwindling as exhaustion takes hold, but I continue to be loud and aggressive in the hope someone will help, but no one does.

People pass by without looking at me, or they're horrified but don't intervene. What the hell?

Are they just going to let this happen?

"Stop fucking screaming."

The voice from behind me belongs to Tommy. It isn't his command that silences me but the relief that I'm not being abducted by an enemy. That feeling is short-lived when I twist to look at him.

If possible, he looks even harder than the last time I saw him. There's no hint of a smile or humour in his eyes as he glowers at me. Every bone in my body flexes as my flight response kicks in once more. But I can't go anywhere. I'm bound and held in the grasp of a man who has iron hands.

"Untie me right now," I demand in a shaky voice.

I'm frazzled and completely terrified by what's going on.

Tommy steps closer to me, and I'm struck by how much he has become one of them. No more jeans and band tees. He's wearing a black coat that reaches his mid-thigh, a dark top underneath, and black trousers with smart shoes. The silver buckle on his belt catches the lights surrounding us, its surface polished to perfection. His hair is slicked back, and the way he's holding himself suggests a confidence I've never seen from him before.

"Put her in the car," he says, though not to me. He's commanding the men around him.

"Tommy, stop!" I struggle against the man holding me as he steps us towards the nearest vehicle. "Wait!"

He glares at me, his lips pulling into a sneer. "For once in your life, do as you're fucking told, Skye."

I lose some of my fight as I'm marched over to the car. Betrayal burns through me like acid as I see Scarlett standing a distance away, her arms folded over her chest as she smirks at me.

I want to smack that look off her face, but I'm pushed into the back of a car, the door shut behind me. A guard takes position on the other side, blocking my view, but not before I see Tommy walk over to Scarlett.

My shoulders hurt the way they are pulled back, but that pain is nothing compared to the agony of knowing my friend sold me out for a guy.

I close my eyes, trying to breathe through the anger. I'm no longer scared. For all this show of force, I know my father won't allow them to hurt me. This is about making a point to me that I'm not the one in control. He is.

The door opens on the other side of where I'm sitting, and Tommy slips inside. Another man gets in the driver seat, but he ignores him, leaning across me to grab my seatbelt.

The way he invades my space isn't as comfortable as it would have been in the past. It only adds to the violation I already feel. Once I'm safely belted in, he sits back in his seat, his thumb rubbing his bottom lip as the engine starts.

His gaze roams over me, no doubt taking in my dishevelled appearance. He doesn't like what he sees either because his jaw tightens, but he says nothing. The silence is worse than being yelled at.

"Where are you taking me?"

He turns to glare at me. "Home."

"I don't want to go home."

"Tough shit."

His tone pisses me off. "I'm not a child, Tommy. I'm the same age as you. I don't deserve to be tied up and dragged into a fucking car."

His fingers lash out, grabbing my chin so hard, I whimper. His eyes are furious as he scans my face. "You're lucky your dad told us not to fucking hurt you."

When he releases me, he shoves me back, and I hit the side door, bruising my shoulder. "Why are you being like this?"

I use my upper body strength to straighten myself, but I wish my hands were free because I'd hit him so hard.

"Do you have any idea where you are?"

"I've been here before."

"Yeah, Skye, before the Sons took control of this area. If you'd run into one of them—" He breaks off, his whole face contorting as he struggles to find control.

Too late.

I did run into one of them. His cock was inside my body less than ten minutes ago, and his leaky condom too. How the hell am I going to get to a pharmacy now?

I jiggle my left leg, nervous energy flowing through me. As soon as I speak to my father, I'm telling him I'm moving into my own place. I can't do this shit anymore. I can't have my life controlled like this.

"I didn't know it was Sons territory. I don't keep up with your enemies, Tommy. We came here because we know the bar and we like it."

He grunts. "You'd have died for your stupidity then. What the fuck are you even doing here, Skye? What are you trying to prove?"

I pin him with my eyes. "Believe it or not, this isn't about proving anything. It's about me getting my life back while you and Dad are off playing fucking soldiers. I want to get a job, and I want to have friends and go to parties."

"You have friends."

My gaze goes to the window as I scoff at him. Buildings whizz past the car, people going about their normal lives. I envy them that.

"Do I? You left, and I don't recognise the person you are now. And Scarlett? Don't get me started on that backstabbing bitch."

"Don't blame her for your bad choices. She called me because she couldn't find you and she was terrified you'd been taken."

Yeah, right!

"She called you because she hates me, Tommy."

"You say I've changed? I don't know who you are either. Scar's been a good friend to you. Better than I have. I can admit that."

"Scarlett wants to fuck you. She doesn't care about me. The only thing she's bothered about is that I'm standing in her way of getting what she wants." I wiggle my wrists, trying to free myself from my bindings, but they're tight around the bones. "Why am I tied up?"

"Because you were acting like a feral bitch. They had to restrain you, Skye, to protect themselves."

I laugh, but there's not a modicum of humour in it. "I didn't realise the Pioneers bred men incapable of handling one little girl."

"Shut up," he snaps, the last vestiges of his patience gone.

"You shut up," I fire back. "You're a fucking dick."

He turns to face me, his gaze sliding towards the man driving, and I know I've stepped over some line I don't know exists. I should shut my mouth, but I don't want to. I'm fuming at him and Scarlett. At my dad too.

"You get a pass because your dad is Desmond Richardson, but don't mistake my leniency for kindness."

Is he serious right now? "Leniency? Where exactly did you show that? When your men were chasing me and scaring me half to death? Or when I was shoved onto the front of a car and tied up? Or was it even before that, when Scarlett was ratting me out to you in the hopes of making you her boyfriend?"

His brows furrow and irritation creases his face. "I don't give a fuck about Scarlett. She's nothing to me. *You are*. If anything had happened to you..."

The way his voice breaks hits my chest like a jackhammer. He reaches out, his fingers cupping my face as his eyes soften.

Oh, shit. Scarlett was right. He *loves* me, and not like a brother. I see the desire, the need in his eyes, and I don't know what the fuck to do with that. I've never felt that way about Tommy. He's my best friend. He's family. But he's not mine, not like that.

My throat burns with my attempt to hold back my emotions because I know my rejection is going to hurt him. I know this because somewhere beneath this façade he wears, the Tommy I know is in there.

Gently, I pull out of his grasp and watch his confusion before he drops his hands. "I don't... I'm not..." I swallow my excuses. There's nothing I can say that will soften this blow. "I love you, Tommy, I always will… but not like that."

The way his softness morphs into granite hardness is alarming. He turns to face the window, and I open my mouth before shutting it again.

What can I say to him?

I focus my attention out the window next to me, trying to work out where we're going. I expect to be taken to Dad's apartment suite, since it's in the city centre, close to where we are now. But as we head farther out, I realise I'm being taken back to the house.

"I don't want to go back there," I say as I see the signs for Dudley. "Stop the car."

"No," Tommy says.

"You can't force me to live there."

"Can't I? You're acting like you have the power in this situation, Skye. You don't."

The back of my neck feels clammy as I stare at him. "You'll have to lock me up to keep me there."

"Then that's what we'll do."

The world around me is still moving, but I feel like I've stopped in place. "You can't hold me prisoner." He doesn't respond. "Tommy!"

"Stop talking."

I sink back, defeated by his callousness. My mind fractures into a million thoughts, and I don't know which one to grab as panic sits like a lump in my throat.

It doesn't take long for the familiar driveway I've used a thousand times to come into view. This time, coming home doesn't feel safe and warm. I feel the chains around my wrists and ankles shackling me to this place.

I glance at Tommy as the car stops in front of the house. Behind us, two other vehicles pull in, and I watch as Scarlett climbs out of the nearest one.

Fucking bitch.

"I'm not staying here with her. I want to speak to my dad."

"He's busy."

"I don't care. Get him on the phone."

Tommy gets out the car, ignoring my protests, and walks around to my side. He pauses for a moment, as if trying to ask the universe for patience before he opens the door.

He grabs me under the back of my bicep, hoisting me out the car. I don't know if it's because my centre of gravity is in the wrong place or if it's nerves, but my legs almost give out on me. He steadies me, and for a second, I see a flash of the boy beneath the man.

"Okay?" he asks, dipping his head to check while his grip keeps me in place.

"What do you care?" I can't help from biting back the words.

"I care, bug. I wouldn't be here if I didn't."

I flinch at his name for me. It used to bring me joy, but now, it just hurts. "Don't call me that."

He blows out a breath. "In time, you'll understand why this has to happen. You can't be out there alone. It's dangerous."

"What about my stuff? It's still at the hotel."

"It's on the way here."

Scarlett really had told them everything. I glare at her from across the driveway, but she doesn't react, and Tommy urges me forwards, changing my attention.

I can do nothing as he leads me into the house, his grip on my arm secure enough to stop me from running. Once we're inside, he orders me to turn around. I don't want to comply, as every fibre of my being wants to argue against every demand he issues, but when two of the guards step towards me, I give in. I don't want their hands on me.

He cuts the rope from my wrists, and my shoulders burn as they return to their natural position. The skin around my wrists is red with blood stains. Tommy takes hold, turning them to examine the damage.

"You shouldn't have fought."

"Would you have come easily?" I snap, tearing out of his hold.

He doesn't answer, which is an answer itself. "You're to stay in the house. A guard will be with you at all times."

I bite my bottom lip so hard, I taste blood. "No. This is not happening."

I try to push around him, but he grabs my shoulders, shoving me into the wall behind me. The world stops for a second, my heart too. In all the years I've known him, he's never put his hands on me. I stare wide-eyed at him, trying to make sense of this stranger in front of me. I want to speak, to say something, but my throat is so tight, I can't form any sounds.

"You'll stay in the house," he repeats. "You can go to the stables, but only with an escort. You will have a guard on you at all times. He will stand outside your bedroom all night while you sleep. He will sit with you at breakfast and dinner. If you try to leave, he has instructions to keep you here by whatever means necessary."

Tears prick my eyes, and I don't try to stop them from falling. "Tommy, please, don't do this to me."

He doesn't meet my gaze, almost as if he can't. "I love you, Skye, but what you did was reckless and beyond crazy. This is for your own good."

He leaves through the front door, and I rush after him, catching it before it swings closed. He doesn't stop despite me calling after him and gets into the car we vacated moments ago.

I try to go to him, but a hand snags around my arm like a vice. I twist to see a tall man towering over me. There's no chinks in his defences. He will drag me back inside and force me to remain here.

I don't fight, knowing it's pointless, and instead turn to watch as Tommy drives away. Scarlett smiles at me, but it's not a nice gesture. Nausea climbs up my throat as I drag myself free and rush into the house.

Grabbing the landline phone from the cradle, I dial 9-9-9. Before the call connects, Scarlett grabs the phone from me and launches it up the hallway. It fractures into pieces, scattering across the floor.

"You're not allow to make calls," she says.

"Why are you doing this? You're supposed to be my friend."

The air between us feels thick and heavy, wrong, and that fear I didn't have with Tommy is here now with Scarlett. "Oh, sweet, stupid Skye. You had everything and never realised it for a moment. I would die for your life."

"You can have it."

"Tommy knows now where my loyalty lies." She leans into me, pushing my hair off my face with her fingertips. "It's always been with him, but now, he knows it."

I swallow down the fear lodged in my throat. "I can't stay here. I need…"

I need medication.

"What do you need, sweetheart?" Her words are kind, but her tone drips with derision. She has all the power here and she knows it. "I can get you whatever you want."

I close my eyes, not wanting to tell her this. I don't trust her, but the morning after pill has to be taken quickly to work. "Can you get me the morning after pill?"

She laughs, and when I don't say anything, she puts a hand to her chest. "Oh, you're serious? You had sex? Where? In the bar?"

I don't answer. I don't owe her that. "Can you get it or not?"

Scarlett grabs my face between her fingers. "Tommy thinks you're this perfect little angel who can do no wrong. Tonight showed him how that view is wrong." Her other hand presses against my stomach. I try to move away, but her hold on my face keeps me in place. "No, Skye, I can't get you the morning after pill. I like the idea of Tommy seeing your belly full with someone else's baby and knowing what a dirty little whore you are."

I see red at her words and spit in her face. It's disgusting, and I can't believe I do it, but I have nothing left in me. "Fuck you," I hiss. "I'm not a whore."

She releases me, and I stagger back, tugging my dress down as if the weight of her accusation layers my skin in filth.

"You had unprotected sex with someone in that bar who I'm guessing you didn't know before tonight. What else should I call you?"

Anger swells in my chest, and I can't stop the snarl from contorting my expression. "I don't have to explain anything to you."

"No, Skye, you don't, but you're not getting out of this house to get rid of whatever mistake you made tonight. I guess we'll see in a few weeks if you're pregnant." She laughs again. "I can't wait for Tommy to see you for what you really are. First, you fuck his brother, and now this? I'm going to bed. It's been a… difficult day. I suggest you do the same."

She heads for the stairs, walking up them as if she owns the place. The man sent to guard me stands against the wall in silence, a sentinel meant to keep watch but not interfere.

A vision of ramming a knife into his gut fills my mind before it flickers away.

Knowing it's hopeless, I make my way upstairs to my room. He follows me, though he doesn't come inside when I close the door behind me. I turn into the room, taking in my bed and the personal effects I left behind.

My room was an expression of me, but now, it's a cell,

designed to keep me locked away. I slide down the door to the floor and draw my knees to my chest.

I should cry. I want to, but the emotion I feel isn't despair—it's red-hot fury. Scarlett, Tommy… they're all going to die. I don't know how or when, but I'm going to make it happen, even if it kills me in the process.

CHAPTER 12
RAGE

"She's so cute."

I glance over as Ophelia waggles a finger in front of the baby's face. Trick's daughter has that chubbiness that all babies have and a dark fuzz of hair covering her crown. I didn't know Mara well, but everyone comments that she's already her mother in miniature. I don't know how a baby can look like anyone. They all look the fucking same.

Ophelia smiles as Sophia reaches out a hand, trying to grab for it, her wide blue eyes in a constant state of what looks like wonderment.

I don't dislike kids, but I'm not interested in playing uncle to the growing gaggle of club brats either. I know a lot of the brothers naturally step into that role, especially once they have their own, but I'm not the guy you trust with the most precious thing in your life. I ain't exactly a great role model for young minds.

"She is cute," Heidi agrees, pulling down the baby's

shirt to cover her belly. "Even when she's screaming at three o'clock in the morning."

I don't know much about women and kids, but the old ladies in London were pushing out babies every other month, or so it seemed. The way Heidi's looking at Sophia is how those mothers looked at their children. That absolute devotion and love is in her eyes.

She ain't seeing Trick and Mara's daughter anymore. That kid is hers, and that ain't good news for anyone. What the fuck happens when Trick finally pulls his head out of his arse and realises he wants Sophia back? What happens when Heidi is relegated back to being Crow's widow and that child is taken from her?

I see the train wreck before it happens. Heidi will have to step back from that kid, hand her over to a man who abandoned her, and go back to being… *what?*

What the fuck does she do?

She's been that baby's mother from the moment she was born, and I don't see her giving up without a fucking fight.

Not my circus, not my monkeys.

This ain't a problem I can solve.

Ophelia catches my gaze as she glances up. "Do you know how long Madden's going to be?"

I shift my shoulders.

Madden—Brewer, as he's known to the club—is out with Terror, looking into a lead on Trick. He was spotted two days ago, just outside of our territory, by a contact of Howler's. I don't know why the fuck they've gone there. It's pointless. Trick will be long gone, probably searching for his next victim. He's really stepping up the Pioneer body count lately, which pisses me off. That shit doesn't come back on him. No one knows where he is, so it's the club that gets hit. It's the old ladies, the kids, and our brothers who are put in danger because of his fucking crusade.

Fuck Trick.

Fuck him and every fucking dickhead in this building who still supports him. It shows growth because I keep those thoughts to myself rather than spilling them.

"You don't say much," Heidi murmurs, her focus still on Sophia.

"Ain't got much to say," I counter, shifting on the bar stool.

The women in this club are in my shit all the time since I saved Hawk and Blackjack from machete-wielding maniacs.

"At least now we know why they call you Rage," she says around a smile.

I make a low grunt in the back of my throat. I've been Rage for only a short time, but that uncontrollable anger has been with me a lot longer.

"I'm grateful you were there," Ophelia adds. "Hawk and Blackjack are good men. It would have been unimaginable losing them."

They are good men.

I'm not.

"Just did my job." This conversation needs to end. I don't want to get into this shit. I don't need praise for killing a man to protect another, but neither of them look like they're going to drop it.

"Is it true they had machetes?"

I side-glance Ophelia, wondering how the fuck to answer her. The club doesn't like shit being shared, and Brew might not appreciate me putting fear into his old lady.

"Doesn't matter what they had," Heidi interjects before I can answer. "If they want you dead, they'll make you dead. That's what happened to my old man."

There's a twist of sadness in her words. I don't know the story behind how she became widowed, but all the brothers in the Manchester chapter wear a patch for Crow, a fallen comrade. I don't, not because I don't want to, but because I ain't earned that right. I didn't know Crow.

"I don't know when Brewer'll be back," I say, hoping it'll stop the questions.

"Is it different here compared to London?"

Fuck. Me.

I grit my teeth. Losing my shit at an old lady is a good way to eat a knuckle sandwich, and probably not just from Brew. The women are treated with reverence in this club. "Not really."

"I've met some of the London boys," she muses. "They're nice."

I snort. Nice ain't the word I'd use. I've seen those men in action, seen them torture and kill in the name of the patch. I've hosed down Fury after he gutted a man, washing every drop of blood from his skin. I've held men down while Nox beat them to death.

They might be soft with their women, with their kids, but they ain't nice.

"I wouldn't say that to them." Heidi pulls out a towel from the nappy bag at her feet and wipes Sophia's face.

I try to hide my disgust. I don't know how babies end up so full of snot and spit.

Ophelia's eyes flare. "Oh! I didn't mean any disrespect."

"You're new to this world," Heidi soothes, "but these men have reputations, and they like to keep them. Don't be telling people they're *nice*."

"Right." She forces an embarrassed smile. "Gotcha. No nice."

I'm debating if it's too early to start drinking just to drown out their conversation.

"How's things with you and Brewer?"

I do not want to hear this. More times than I can count, I've accidentally overheard something about one of the brothers that made me want to bleach my brain.

"Amazing. He's so good to me."

I'm about to slip off my stool when Heidi says, "What about you, Rage? Anyone catching your eye?"

The mischievous glint in her eyes tells me she knows exactly what she's doing. I don't need or want to be involved in fucking girl chat, but my mind drifts to the woman I fucked in Lassiter's office.

Skye.

Every inch of her was perfect. Her cunt had squeezed my

dick so hard, I thought I was going to pass out as I sunk into her depths. The way she'd looked with my fingers wrapped in her hair is emblazoned on my brain. I'll never forget those little moans she made, the way she thrust back to meet me, and how heavy her eyes were after I slid free of her.

She was a world away from the club bunnies and hangarounds I've been with in the past. It's a pity she was such a stuck-up bitch. It ruins my memory of that night. I'm used to those mistrustful looks, even fear, but her expression had been pure terror.

Movement across the room catches my attention as Hawk steps through the doors. He scans the room, spotting me, and crooks two fingers in my direction. Grateful for the interruption, I slide off my chair and cross the room.

"What's up?" I dig my fists into my jeans pockets as I approach him.

He's tense, his shoulders tight, and that puts me on edge. He gestures for me to follow him out the room, and once the common room door is shut behind us, he speaks. "Ain't had a chance to talk to you since you got back from Birmingham. How was it?"

"It was… weird."

His brows draw down. "Weird how?"

How the fuck do I explain the unease I felt being there? Most people deal in absolutes, but my life being the way it has been, I trust that inbuilt instinct I have. A gut feeling has saved me more times than I can count.

"There was an atmosphere. I went on a job with Nicky, but even before that, he was sitting outside guarding the gate. He's wearing an SAA patch and watching the entrance."

Hawk's heavy brows draw together. "Nicky's SAA now?"

"That's what the patch said."

I don't know if that's good or bad news. I can't read Hawk's expression, which I don't like. "Did Crank say or do anything?"

"No, but Nicky was worried about some girl named Chloe he's fucking. Said she was trouble." This expression there's no mistaking. He's pissed. "Who is she?"

He steps away, pacing with his hands on his hips. "He definitely said Chloe?"

"Yeah." I don't know what her importance is, but clearly, it's hit a nerve.

"Her mum was a club whore. I don't think there was a member in that whole chapter who hadn't sampled her at least half a dozen times. She got pregnant, and I think she realised she couldn't raise a kid in that environment.

"She was never gonna be seen as anything but a club whore and she knew it. She left the club when Chlo was maybe three or four weeks old. Chlo was maybe twelve the first time she came to the clubhouse. Grub wanted her gone, but she came back. She was curious to know where she came from." He pulls his mouth into a snarl. "That girl wants to get her hooks into a brother. She's got this idea that she needs to be more than her mum was, that by being an old lady, she'll right the wrongs of the past. But Stella left to give that girl a good life. She never wanted her daughter to be on the back of anyone's saddle, and she definitely wouldn't have wanted her daughter shacking up with fucking Crank."

I'm a piece of shit who has done some really questionable things in my time, but something about all that sits wrong with me. "Ain't a chance that he's her dad, is there?"

Why's that the first thing that enters my fucking head?

"No. Crank wasn't at Birmingham then, and it was long before my time."

"Well, Crank's fucking her."

His mouth tears into a grimace. "Ain't surprised. He's a piece of shit excuse for a man. Makes sense he'd want to fuck someone young and easily impressed. Did Nicky say anything else?"

I shake my head. "He took me on a job to some bar." *Where I fucked the brains out of a girl called Skye.* "I didn't see him after we got back to the clubhouse. Hawk… you trusted me with something big." The way he's looking at me makes me wish I hadn't fucking started this.

"I told you, you're one of us."

"I know, but it meant a lot to me that you didn't just say those words. You showed me."

"I want you to stay here, kid. We all do." He winces, rubbing the back of his neck suddenly, as if he doesn't want to say the next words. "Wren… she, um… wanted to ask you over for dinner. I told her it wouldn't be your thing, but she won't let it go. You saved my arse, and she thinks the way to show her gratitude is to feed you."

Oh, fuck. I can't think of a single thing I'd like to do less. "Seriously?"

"You don't go, she's gonna keep giving me shit about it. Just say yes."

I would rather scoop my eyes out with a rusty spoon.

"Fine, but you owe me."

He sighs. "Believe me, kid, one day, you'll have an old lady and you'll do anything to make her happy."

I doubt it, but I don't say anything. I don't go back to the bar, either. Instead, I head up to my room and strip out of my clothes. I'm lucky to have a room with its own bathroom. The shared shower down the hall is disgusting, even by my standards. Once I've run the water and it's hot, I step under the spray.

I run my fingers through my hair as the water cascades over me.

Skye...

Fuck Heidi for bringing that memory to the front of my mind. I can't think of anything but her as I take my cock in a soapy hand. Closing my eyes, I imagine it's her touch on my shaft as I slowly move my fingers up and down. I can't stop the little grunt that sounds in the back of my throat as my balls tighten.

Drawing in air through my nose, I place my free hand against the tile and work my shaft. I keep focused on her face behind my closed lids, my body tight and prepping for release.

I imagine lying her back and playing with her nipples as she stares at me through thick lashes. My hand keeps moving insistently on my cock, my balls growing heavier by the second. Fuck, I'm not going to last long.

Her sweet voice calls my name, and it's enough to send

me over the edge. My body releases the tension I'm holding on to, and I spill cum over my hand and onto the tile in front of me.

Stars spill through my vision, and I swear I see double for a moment before it clears.

It pisses me off I'm thinking about her when she clearly hates me, but some women are hard to forget. She's one of them.

Fucking Skye...

CHAPTER 13
SKYE

The metallic scrape of the lock on my door sliding back is enough to pull me from the restless sleep I'm in. Jack-knifing up, shoving aside my tiredness, I tug the duvet around my body as if it can protect me from whatever acid Scarlett will spew at me this morning.

She has been insufferable since I was brought home and locked within these four walls, a prisoner in a place that was once my sanctuary.

There's no peace for me, not here, not anymore. The chains might be imaginary, but they're tight around my body as I prepare to face the woman who has become my greatest enemy.

It scares me how easily she was able to hide her hatred for me over the years. Did it fester away from the moment we became friends, or was it more recently that her mood towards me changed?

Those questions have been circling my brain all day

long as I try to make sense of the situation I find myself in.

My body is tight as the door to my bedroom opens and she steps inside, clutching a small paper bag. The smile she gives me is laced with so much disdain, it's hard not to recoil from her.

"Rise and shine, *Skye-bug*."

Her words are designed to cut, to make me bleed mentally. It's a taunt of the past, a reminder that the life I knew no longer exists. I'm at her mercy every moment of the day with no one to help or protect me.

Time has passed slowly, agonisingly so. I'm losing all sense of rationality with each hour I'm forced to remain within these four walls. The house that once held all my best memories has become the very thing that is unravelling me thread by thread.

I don't even look at her as I throw my covers back and sit on the edge of my bed. The light changes in the room as she tugs back the curtains, letting the sunlight stream inside. It feels warm on my back, but it doesn't chase the cold away.

"I want to speak to my dad," I say.

I've asked this question multiple times, but the answer is always the same. At first, I didn't want to believe my father endorsed this, but the more time that passes, the further that hope slips. He hasn't contacted me or come to the house to see if I'm okay. Those actions tell me everything.

He doesn't care, and I'm alone in facing these demons.

And Scarlett *is* a demon.

She has taken great pleasure in keeping me down and tormenting me. The use of 'Skye-bug' is just one example of this. She knows what that nickname means to me. Tommy loved me enough to give me it, even if he no longer cares about me.

That has to piss Scarlett off.

She is completely in love with him, to the point I think she would kill me if I stood between them.

Lucky for me, the only feelings I have for Tommy right now are anger. His betrayal of me is just as bad as Scarlett's.

"Did you hear me?" She doesn't answer this time either, which makes me grind my teeth together.

"I heard, but since you know what the answer will be, I don't see the point in saying it."

No, she wouldn't.

"I'm done playing this fucking game, Scarlett. I'm leaving, and the only way you're going to stop me is by killing me."

I slip off the bed and stuff my feet in the running shoes against the wall. She doesn't react to my outburst, which should make me hesitant, but I'm so done.

I open the door only to be greeted by a mountain of a man blocking the frame. He turns to look at me before glancing behind me towards Scarlett.

"Move." He doesn't, so I slam my fist into his back as hard as I can.

Twisting around, he grabs my wrists, and with a strength that I could never match, he pushes me back into my bedroom. I fight with everything I have, trying desperately to free myself from his hold, but the bed hits the back of my legs as I'm forced onto it.

For a flash of a moment, I panic that he's going to force himself on me, but he releases his grasp as soon as I'm immobilised.

"You can wait outside, Harry," she tells him.

How is she on first name terms with my captors? I don't recognise half the men who guard me like rabid dogs.

He glances down at me before crossing the room and stepping back out onto the landing. I scramble up out of that vulnerable position and try to calm my rage. How dare he! How dare she!

As soon as the door is closed, an image of Scarlett's bleeding throat flashes through my mind. Despite the world I live in, I'm not a violent person, and I have never craved the darkness that surrounds those around me, but killing her is fast becoming the only thought I can hold on to. I don't know how I'm going to do it, or when, but there is no world I can exist in that allows her to keep breathing.

"Thinking about murdering me again?"

Her nonchalance doesn't surprise me. She thinks I'm this weak, helpless girl, and although Harry just proved strength-wise I am, there are other ways to be strong. My resolve remains unbroken. I want to escape. I want to reclaim my life. The determination I feel is a constant burning inside me that cannot be extinguished.

"I think about murdering you every second of the day."

I'm scared of the intrusive thoughts that live in my head since Tommy dragged me home and forced this prison on me. I don't just think about killing the woman who used to be my friend, I come up with more and more inventive ways to do it.

Scarlett's smirk pisses me off. She thinks I'm full of bluster, that my words are empty threats. She couldn't be more wrong. The first opportunity I have, I'm ending her fucking life.

Oblivious to the dark path of my thoughts, she drops the paper bag on the end of the bed, gesturing for me to take it.

I stare at it for a moment before lifting my gaze to hers. "What's that?"

"A pregnancy test. I think it's time to do one, don't you?"

I stare at the bag like it's live ammunition. I don't need a test to tell me I'm pregnant. I'm not the kind person who plays Russian roulette with a broken condom and doesn't get the bullet. One mistake on my part is always going to end with the worst possible outcome. Besides, I've always found the universe has a funny sense of humour, and having the baby of my father's enemy is the greatest joke the cosmos can pull.

I try to ignore the tremble of anxiety that works through my body as a thousand scenarios play in my brain, each one ramping up my fear even higher.

What if I am pregnant?

What happens to me, and to my baby, if I'm forced to have this child?

What if Scarlett, my father, or Tommy discover who I slept with?

I wish I could go back to that night and undo all the damage I've caused, but as far as I know, time travel isn't possible. This is the hand I've been dealt, and all I can do is play my cards… however bad they may be.

"I don't want to take the test." I fold my arms over my chest, glaring at her.

"Have you had your period yet?"

I don't answer. She knows I haven't because she's checked every fucking day since I told her I needed the morning after pill. It's been five weeks since that night, and I've not bled once in that time. I don't know much about pregnancy, but I'm pretty sure that's a bad sign.

"I take it that's a no then." Scarlett pulls the packet out of the bag and thrusts it in my direction. "It can't hurt to take it and find out for sure."

It can't hurt her, but it can most definitely hurt me. "I'm not pregnant, Scarlett. I haven't had any symptoms." If I am, I don't know what my next step is. "I'm not taking the test."

"Either you do it or I'll have a doctor come to the house. If we have to do it that way, I'll have Harry pin you down while the doctor gets whatever they need from you."

Fucking. Bitch.

My anger is so potent, I could rip her limb from limb with my bare hands. "One day, I'm going to kill you, Scarlett."

"Maybe, but today is not that day, Skye. Take the fucking test. If you're… with child," she waves her hand at my stomach, disgust curling her mouth, "then we need to know. You'll need medications and check-ups. Proper nutrition. We wouldn't want anything to happen to your baby, would we?"

The threat in her words doesn't bypass me. I don't even know if I am pregnant, but an overprotective urge surges through me. I don't think. I lash out, smashing my fist into the side of her face. I'm not ashamed at the amount of satisfaction I experience as she stumbles, grabbing the bedrail at the end of the mattress to keep her feet. She screams for Harry as I strike again, hitting her with every ounce of strength I possess. Blood sprays from her mouth as her head snaps to the side.

I almost roar with triumph. Weeks of pent-up rage flow through me like a turbulent river.

Fuck. You. *Bitch*.

I'm going to beat her bloody.

I'm going to—

Thick arms wrap around me from behind, dragging me back. I shriek, kicking my legs and fighting like a demon. I'm going to destroy her.

Harry moves me away from Scarlett as she clamours to her feet, wiping blood from her lips. "You fucking cunt," she snarls at me.

The steel bands of Harry's arms wrapped around me stop me from protecting myself as she hits me hard enough to rattle my teeth. The force nearly takes my head off my neck.

Pain burns through my jaw and cheek, the bone aching like it's made of stone.

"You're lucky you're in a… delicate situation," she hisses at me before nodding at Harry.

He releases his hold on me, and I stumble away from them both. "You get my father on the phone right now."

"You can wait outside, Harry. But don't go far," she adds, which makes me smirk.

"Worried I'm going to hit you again?" I ask, breathing hard as the door is shut again, leaving me alone with a psycho.

"More worried I might need him to pull me off you." She retrieves the box from the floor, and I wonder if Harry saw it, or if any of my guards are telling my father the things I am enduring here. "Take the fucking test, Skye. Don't you want to know?"

"It might not even work," I say. "It was only five weeks ago."

"But it might. Do you want Harry to make you do it?"

Reluctantly, I reach out and take it from her. I don't know that I want the truth here, but no one in this house is on my side, so I believe Scarlett when she says Harry will force me to take the test.

I step into my bathroom, closing the door behind me. My heart is thudding as I pull out the leaflet and read the instructions. Once I have that in my head, I sit on the toilet and do the test.

After I've finished, I cap the stick and place it on the side of the basin while I wash my hands. I don't ever think I've been this scared in my entire life.

I close my eyes, trying to breathe through the swelling panic in my gut as the seconds tick by.

Whatever happens, it'll be okay.

I'll make sure it's okay.

I open my eyes and glance down at the little window in the test. Nothing yet. Shit.

Banging on the door makes me jump. "Have you done it yet?"

I grit my teeth. I don't want her anywhere near me. Catching my reflection in the mirror, I notice the redness on my cheek where she hit me. The skin already feels like it's stretched tight over the bone, and I'm sure it'll bruise tomorrow.

"Fuck off," I yell at the door.

It feels like the wait lasts an eternity, but then a line appears. I grab the instructions, reading them as I watch the test work. One line is good. It means the test is negative.

Then I spot a very faint second line. It's so faint, I'm not sure if it's really there. Holding it closer to my face, I try to see it clearer.

Is that... is that a second line?

I lick my suddenly dry lips, the only sound my own ragged breathing as it darkens a little. It's still faint, but it's there. I'm not imagining it.

Two lines on a pregnancy test.

It's positive.

I'm pregnant with a stranger's baby. Nausea swamps me, a sticky heat scorching my skin as the realisation of my predicament settles in.

I'm pregnant.

I suspected, of course I did—the condom broke while we were having sex, so this was always a chance—but this isn't suspicion now. It's reality.

My thoughts are chaotic as I try to make sense of what I'm facing. I can't have a baby. I'm eighteen years old, barely an adult myself.

And you don't even know the name of your baby's father.

Oh *fuck*.

I'm going to vomit.

I drop to my knees in front of the toilet as my stomach contracts savagely. Bile coats my throat as I retch and my body tries to expel everything I ate last night.

Nothing comes up, but the wave of nausea continues to wash over me.

"Skye? Are you okay?"

I want to laugh. Like she fucking cares if I'm okay. Another wave of nausea has me gagging again, and all thoughts of Scarlett flee as I try to control my stomach.

I knew this was a possibility, that without the medication I needed I could end up this way, but realising how my life is about to change has me weighed down with dread.

Sinking back from the toilet, I sag against the wall next to me, hopelessness swarming over me as my hand rests over my stomach.

I can't do this.

I'm not strong enough to be a mother.

There is a gnawing ache as I wish, and not for the first

time, that my mother was here. She would never have allowed Dad to treat me like this. She'd also know what to do about my little 'problem'.

I don't know how I'm meant to feel. I want to be a mum, but not at eighteen and not like this. I'm not ready.

I'm also a captive in my own home.

The uncertainty about my future only fuels the wild anxiety threatening to drown me.

"Skye! Open the door!"

I get to my feet, my legs shaky, and tear the door open, blowing past Scarlett. I don't know what to do, where to turn. Tommy has always been my go-to.

"Are you pregnant?"

"This could have been prevented," I yell, unable to control the tremble working through me. "You spiteful bitch. How could you do this to me?"

Her mouth curves into a smile. "You are. You're pregnant."

"Don't look so fucking happy about it."

I need to get in touch with my father somehow. I need to find a way out of here. It's early enough I can terminate the pregnancy.

Even as I think that, I don't like how it makes me feel. This baby might be half a biker, but it's also half me. Can I really have an abortion?

I shake myself mentally.

I have to. I'm a teenager with no money and zero means of taking care of a child. If I manage to gain my freedom, I'll be running for the rest of my life.

What kind of existence is that for a kid?

My chest suddenly feels tight, each breath a chore to drag into my pained lungs.

"Perfect Skye," Scarlett mutters, "no longer the golden one. What do you think Tommy and your dad are going to think about this?"

"I don't care what either of them think. I don't care what you think either, and you can't hold me here forever."

Her head tilts to the side. "Can't I? I mean, you're free to try to leave. Harry might give you a head start, but in your condition, I don't think I'd put myself in a position where a grown man is likely to body slam me to the ground."

I rub at my sternum, trying to dispel the growing discomfort there. "All I've ever done is be your friend. If you wanted Tommy, you could've just said. I would have happily celebrated your relationship. You didn't have to stick a knife in my back when I wasn't looking."

"You should come eat breakfast," she says, ignoring my rebuke. "You're eating for two now. You need to keep your strength up."

She walks to the door, and as she reaches for the handle, I speak. "I can't kill you today, probably not tomorrow or even the next day, but one thing you seem to have forgotten, Scarlett, is that I am a Richardson, and I am my father's daughter. Enjoy what time you have left."

The smirk she gives me only fuels my need to end her life even more brutally than I've imagined. "Don't take too long."

As soon as I'm alone, I take a steadying breath to calm

the red-hot fury smouldering inside me. I have to escape, but where the hell do I go when I'm free?

There's nowhere I can hide from my father and his Pioneers. Nowhere safe.

Except with him.

The biker.

I dismiss the idea as soon as it enters my head. There's not a chance on this earth that he's going to protect me from this. He's more likely to kill me and send my father body parts as trophies of my murder. Besides, I don't know his name, only his location.

His patch had said Manchester.

Considering I can't even get out the house, how would I get there? I don't have money or a phone, and I doubt Scarlett is going to give me train fare.

The walls feel like they're closing in on me. I'm trapped in a snare that I cannot break free of. Staying is no longer an option. To deal with this *baby issue*, I need to see a doctor, but Scarlett is never going to allow that to happen. She wants me to bear this, to face my sins.

I splay my fingers over my stomach.

I'm sorry, little one, but there's nothing good for you out here.

I sink onto the edge of the bed and bury my head in my hands, wondering what the fuck I'm going to do.

CHAPTER 14
SKYE

The floor is hard beneath my spine despite the plush rug I'm lying on. I trace the patterns on the ceiling above me, humming while I do. I don't know why I've never noticed how ugly the Artex is, but then I've never studied it this closely.

In the past week, I have become intimately acquainted with my bedroom. After I attacked Scarlett, she punished me by locking me away. My freedom narrowed even further to staring at the four walls that had previously been a comfort to me.

I hate her for that most of all.

She has made my childhood home a place of misery and despair.

A wave of nausea rolls through me, and I close my eyes, blocking my bedroom out as I suck air through my nose. I'm six weeks pregnant and yesterday I puked for the first time. I've thrown up plenty of times from drink, rides, even overeating, but that was something else. It came on so suddenly, and I clung to the toilet bowl, hanging on for life. Stupidly, I hoped that would be a one-off event, but from the way my stomach is churning now, I'm guessing not.

I'm hoping it doesn't last long. A week seems reasonable, right?

I hate not knowing what to expect. This shit was never covered in school. Sure, we talked about periods and safe sex, but not one health education class went through what happens when you *are* pregnant.

Usually, I would look to the internet for answers, but Scarlett took away all my means to communicate with the outside world—including my phone, which I left in the hotel room. So, I'm trying to remember any detail I can about pregnancy from films or books I've read.

I recall the morning sickness part, but no one ever mentioned the tiredness or the fact my breasts ache so bad, I barely touch them.

My stomach turns itself inside out, and I taste acid in my throat. This is the worst. Why do they call it morning sickness when it happened all day yesterday?

I hate Scarlett for forcing this upon me. No one wants to have their choices ripped from them, and she has taken every single one from me. I could have dealt with this the same night or even the day after the condom broke. I know in my heart I'm not ready to be a mother; I'm barely an adult myself. I've never lived alone. I've never had a job. This time last year, I was still in school.

Scarlett's vindictiveness is what hurts the most. I had no idea just how much she hates me. Pregnancy isn't something you force on someone else, but the more time that passes, the more difficult it will be for me to remedy this situation. She plans to ruin me because Tommy loves me and not her. It doesn't matter that I don't love him that way. She's past reasoning. All Scarlett sees is her hate for me.

Splaying my hand over my belly, I swallow down another wave of nausea, blowing air through my pursed lips.

How long does this last?

This is torture.

I wonder if I can find that biker just so I can kick his balls into his stomach. He did this to me. His nonchalant 'take care of it' routine still irritates me. How does he get to have sex and walk away without a single risk to him while I'm lying on my bedroom floor trying not to puke?

I bet plenty of women are taken in by that stupid floppy hair and edginess he has. I should have known he was in the life. The way he carried himself, the no-fucks given attitude... I've seen it a hundred times. Jack was a prime example. The swagger was a part of him. He walked into a room and commanded attention. My mysterious biker was the same.

Tommy is getting that way. The last time I saw him, I didn't recognise him at all. He's no longer the boy who used to wake me in the mornings and call me his bug.

And my father? I'm starting to suspect he's dead because I refuse to believe he would leave me here like this and not speak to me. My father has never been a hands-on parent, but he didn't even call to yell at me for running away.

Why?

My father would have ripped me to shreds under normal circumstances, not even out of concern but because he would've found it embarrassing that I left.

I haven't heard a word from him, which means I'm alone and I'm going to have to save myself.

The first thing I need to do when I'm free is find an abortion clinic. I grimace at the thought. It makes the hair stand up on my arms when I think about terminating this baby. I don't know if I can, but how can I continue with this pregnancy?

If by some miracle I manage to escape this prison, then what? I have no money and nowhere to go. All my friends are part of my father's organisation. I don't have family away from this world either. I have a credit card, sure, but it's Dad's account. I'll be traceable the moment I use it. If I go, I need to be completely off the radar to stay safe, and logically, I can't think of a single way to do that.

I might be naive, but I do know something about how the world works.

How do I get a house without a deposit?
How do I get a job without any experience?
How do I stay hidden from Tommy and the Pioneers?

The only person who might be able to help is the biker, whose name I don't know. His club is fighting against my dad. He has the means and the position to protect me, but is that really an option? What happens when he discovers who I really am?

I don't know what the issue is between his club and my father's gang, but I do know the amount of dead on our side suggests there isn't going to be room at the table for the daughter of the man behind this feud.

Escaping this hell only to have my throat slit and my body dumped in a ditch isn't a plan.

So, I'm fucked. There is no hope for me. Everything feels like a monumental challenge.

You can't stay here, Skye.

I want to silence that voice in my head, but it's right. I can't stay. The longer I'm here, the more at risk I am. At the moment, I can run and I can fight, but how can I do that with a pregnant belly in my way at six or seven months?

Scarlett will have complete control over me once I get into that part of my pregnancy. Considering how unhinged she is, I fear what she might do if pushed into a corner. She's already shown me she has no issue hitting me, pregnant or not.

So, I need a plan.

Right after I stop feeling sick.

Draping an arm over my eyes, I try to breathe through the wave of sickness. It's starting to recede, though not fast enough. I struggle to sit up and stumble over to the window, shoving it open and sucking in a lungful of cold air. It helps a little, but it doesn't completely settle my stomach.

I glance down at the patio below. It's a fair drop, and I've wondered more times than I can count if I can make it without breaking all the bones in my legs.

The sound of the lock scraping back has my neck snapping in that direction. I brace, steeling my spine as the door opens and Scarlett steps inside carrying a wooden tray that my mum used before she passed away. It pisses me off that she's found it and is sullying the memory I have of it, but the longer I stand there, the more I realise maybe my mum is helping me from the beyond. Her dad made the tray, carved it for her as a wedding present when she married my dad. It's made from heavy wood, and I could never lift it as a kid. Until seeing it this moment, I forgot we had it.

Like a fucking saint, Scarlett smiles and chatters about the weather as she places the tray on my empty desk—another thing she took, my computer. I get a glimpse of the guard waiting outside before he pulls the door shut.

"You're looking a little green today," she remarks in a way that makes me want to kill her with my bare hands. If I'm green, it's her fucking fault. "Since you've started having morning sickness, I brought you some ginger tea. It's meant to help with nausea."

This *bitch*.

I slam my teeth together so I don't lose my shit at her. I don't respond either. There's no point, and my mind is working overtime, formulating an escape plan.

Oblivious to the dark turn my thoughts have taken, Scarlett gives me a radiant smile as she takes every item off the tray one piece at a time. There's some toast, fruit, and the tea. No cutlery. I've not been allowed to use silverware since I returned here. For all her act, Scarlett is well aware that, given the chance, I'd stab her cold, dead heart.

I watch as she fusses with the items, setting it up on the desk like we're having afternoon tea. When she's satisfied, she steps back, her smile still in place.

"I hope the toast is all right. I didn't think you'd be able to keep anything down but plain food. Make sure you eat everything, though. I've done a lot of reading, and you need the nutrition at this early stage. Baby is growing every day." Her eyes drop to my flat belly, and my hands move to cover myself. I don't know why I feel a wave of protectiveness in this moment. Only minutes ago, I was thinking about abortion, but my instinct is to keep her away from my baby.

Scarlett smirks, as if she's happy to see me uncomfortable. "There's some pre-natal medication too—for the baby." She points to a little glass bowl with a couple pills in. I'm not taking anything she gives me. "You don't have to look so suspicious, Skye. I'm not going to give you anything to harm that precious bundle you're carrying."

"Have you spoken to Tommy or my dad?" I shouldn't ask, but I can't hold my silence any longer.

The expression that ripples across her face scares me. "Tommy's busy, Skye. He doesn't have time to check in on you twenty-four-fucking-seven."

"Clearly, he doesn't have time to check in on you, either."

She licks her lips, her eyes blazing. "You think he cares about you? When he finds out you're pregnant—"

"I don't care if he finds out," I interrupt. "Tommy is nothing to me anymore."

She laughs. "I'm sure he'll be gutted to know that."

I breathe through my nose like a raging bull. I don't care if I never get out this room, but I can't stand another second in this fucking cunt's presence.

"Enjoy your breakfast, Skye."

As she turns back to the door, I see my opportunity. I should wait and have a plan in place, but I'm running on pure anger.

Before I stop to consider what happens if I fail, I grab the tray and move with speed that shouldn't be possible considering how sick I am.

Using every ounce of strength I possess, I swing it and hit the back of her head. The clunk it makes as it connects with her skull makes me even more queasy. She staggers, dazed, but she's not down, and that is my aim.

I raise the tray again, but before I can act, she flashes an arm out, slamming into my stomach hard enough to make me retch.

Fuck.

Instinctively, I come up swinging, ready to protect myself and my baby, but I'm not fast enough before she connects a fist to my cheek. It's not hard, but pain blossoms through the bone anyway. Her movements are uncoordinated enough that it gives me the chance to regain my composure and smack the tray into her skull again.

This time, she goes to her knees. Blood trails from

beneath her hairline as her eyes lift to mine, begging me not to hurt her.

For a moment, I see the girl in floral dresses and pink shoes who used to ride ponies with me and play make-believe in the vast gardens of my family home.

She lurches forwards, as if she's going to strike me. I react on instinct, hitting so hard that her eyes roll in her head, and she slumps to the floor, her legs twisted awkwardly beneath her.

My heart is pounding as I stare down at her body. Did I… did I kill her?

A tremble works through my limbs, my legs feeling jellied. I lean on the baseboard at the end of the bed to steady myself. Scarlett doesn't move, not even an inch. I try to see if her chest is rising and falling, but the angle she's lying in makes it hard to tell.

My pulse flutters frantically in my throat, and the back of my neck is clammy as I stare at her body.

I had to do it.

There was no choice, right?

The entire incident took less than a minute and didn't make enough noise to rouse the guard outside the door. I don't know why, but that bothers me. I killed someone, and no one noticed. The world kept turning for everyone else, apart from Scarlett.

I press my fingers to my aching face. My bruises from the last attack haven't disappeared yet, and now, I'll be adding new ones. I close my eyes for a brief second, trying to calm my racing thoughts and heart.

I'm not free yet. There are other obstacles to get through.

Like the guard.

He isn't going to be as easy to get past. I can't out-muscle him as I'm a fraction of his size. Hitting him with the tray probably won't work.

The window isn't an option, so the only way out of the house is through my bedroom door and past him.

But how?

A sweep of my room doesn't yield anything I can use, until my gaze stops on the tea.

I stare at the steam rising from the top of the mug. Fuck, I don't like this plan. There are too many variables, too many things that can wrong, but I can't stay here either.

Avoiding looking at Scarlett's body, I grab a pair of running shoes from my walk-in and slide my feet into them. I don't bother with socks. There isn't time.

My dark leggings aren't warm, but they are comfortable. The vest top I'm wearing isn't enough, so I grab a sweater and drag it over my head.

I don't bother settling it into place as I grab the mug from my desk, burning my knuckles as they press against the ceramic.

Before I can move, there's a knock on the door before it opens. My heart freezes as the guard takes in the mess and Scarlett curled on the floor, still unmoving.

There's a split second where neither of us react, shocked into immobility. Then he comes at me.

I panic and toss the tea in his face. He recoils, screaming in pain as it burns him, his hands covering where I threw it. I seize the moment of distraction to dart around him and run.

Misjudging my steps, I hit the edge of the door frame as I barrel through it, but I push aside the pain that sings through my shoulder and down my arm. I don't stop as I rush along the landing and grip the banister tightly as I fly down the stairs.

Focus, Skye.

I try to keep my thoughts clear as I run to the drawer in the foyer where all the car keys are kept. When I open it, there's nothing in there.

Fuck.

Scarlett must have moved them.

Movement from above has my neck snapping back. The guard is stumbling along the landing in my direction. I need transport. It's the only way to get out of here.

Think!

My dad has a classic car in the garage, an old vehicle that cost him a small fortune to buy. He keeps the keys in his office… not with the other keys.

I take off at full speed, racing through the house and stopping for a brief second to open the door. Dad's office looks the same as it always has. The large oak desk in the middle of the floor and the dark stained bookshelves that line one wall have remained unchanged for most of my life.

I ignore all of that and rush around the edge of the desk, dragging the top drawer open. There's a pile of shit in there—pens, some stationary, and the keys.

Fuck, yes!

I snatch them up, stuffing them in the pocket on the front of my sweater.

"Can't let you leave, Miss Richardson," a voice says from the doorway.

My head snaps up to find the guard is standing there. I don't know his name, I never asked, and my dad seems to have new guys on rotation all the time, but I do feel slightly bad for the damage I've caused him. His face is red and blistering already, and it must hurt like hell.

"The only way you're going to stop me is to kill me," I tell him, meaning every word.

"I don't want to hurt you."

"Then stay out of my way."

He winces, and I can see in his face he really doesn't want to hurt me. "Can't do that."

I back up to the French doors that look out over the side garden. So many nights my father sat in this room, the doors open, conducting his business. Stealing money, killing men who got in his way, acting every inch the legitimate businessman while funnelling dirt through the area.

I know where the doors are without looking, so as I back up, I don't take my eyes off him.

"Just let me go, please." I don't want to beg, but I'd also prefer not to kill anyone else if I don't have to.

He shakes his head. "I'm sorry. I'm not dying for you."

Despite his injuries, the guard rushes at me. I try to run, but he grabs me by my wrists, shoving me back. I stumble, trying not to lose my footing as he pushes me against the bookshelf behind me. A sharp pain works down my spine as I connect with the wood.

His grasp is like iron, clamping me in place no matter how hard I fight him. The man is huge, his frame completely surrounding me as I thrash against his hold.

I'm not falling at this hurdle, not when freedom is so close, I can almost touch it.

There's just enough room between us for me to bring my knee up. I slam it as hard as I can into his dick, ignoring the way it feels as I make contact.

The noise he makes scores my brain in an unpleasant way. It's a strangled scream, released through a corded throat, but it has the desired effect. He lets go of me to stagger back, gripping between his legs.

As I move past him, he fumbles out with a hand, grabbing my bicep hard enough to leave a bruise. I pull the keys from my pocket, dragging the edge of one down his face. Blood bubbles as he screams again.

I flinch, hating the pain I'm inflicting on him, but there's no time for me to feel remorse. I run from the room, making straight for the front door. Pulling the latch back, I drag it open and pound my feet across the driveway to the garage. As I close in, I fumble with the keys, ignoring the blood on the side of one, and hit the garage door opener. The mechanism kicks in and it rolls up inch-by-inch until it reveals the car. I round the front, fumbling to unlock the driver's door.

I learned to drive as soon as I was able to because of the horses. There are times they need to be transported places, and I didn't want to rely on the stable staff. I've never driven this car before though, so it takes me a moment to familiarise myself with the controls before I shove the key into the ignition.

It's an old car, one of those sporty types from the seventies, and it has a manual choke. I've used one a few times on some of the equipment we use for the horse, so I know what to do, but my nerves get the better of me. It splutters and almost dies on me before I manage to adjust it enough for the engine to purr into action.

Ready to drive, I glance up and see the guard standing in the driveway.

Motherfucker...

There's blood trailing down his blistered face and his eyes are pure fury. He's not stopping me from leaving. Nothing is.

I put the car into gear and hit the accelerator.

As I speed towards him, he doesn't move. I'm going to hit him.

Get out the way...

He doesn't, and before I can stop myself, I slam on the brake, skidding to a stop just feet from him. We lock eyes through the windscreen, the constant thump in my chest so loud, I can feel it against my ribs. I tighten my hold on the steering wheel until my knuckles burn from the skin stretching over them, and as he steps towards the car, towards me, I hit the accelerator.

As he hits the bonnet and flies backwards like a projectile until he falls like a rag doll on the tarmac, I flinch, almost releasing the steering wheel as I hit the brakes. I don't move the car, staring at the spot where he's lying on his side. Is he dead?

I don't know, but I'm not willing to find out if he's still breathing. Closing my eyes, I hit the accelerator.

The car bumps suddenly and I almost vomit knowing I've hit him. My eyes fly open just in time to stop from veering off the driveway.

I don't dare look in the mirror as I drive towards the front entrance of the property. Part of me hopes he's dead, part of me hopes he's not.

I ignore both, rolling the car to a stop at the gate. Where the fuck am I going to go?

To him.

What choice do I have?

This is his baby I'm carrying. I can only hope that means something to him. Maybe that knowledge will allow him to overlook who I am and who he is.

I peer up the road both ways and then make my decision. Checking it's safe, I turn left, heading in the direction I know will take me to Manchester.

CHAPTER 15
RAGE

Another warehouse, another loose thread that leads nowhere. I glance around the room, taking in the exposed brickwork and broken windowpanes. The smell of mould clings to my nose, tickling my senses in an unpleasant way.

Blackjack walks over to the corner, toeing a pile of empty food wrappers, and crouches down. Grabbing a bottle of booze, his mouth pulls into a tight line before he tosses it back onto the concrete. The sound reverberates through the space, echoing off the high ceilings.

"He was here," he mutters, standing and wiping his hands on his jeans.

The tightness of his jaw and the way it ticks as he scans the room tells me everything I need to know. He's pissed, and I don't blame him for that. It feels like we're on an endless chase to catch Trick, yet we're always two steps behind. It's getting annoying.

"Ain't here now," I supply unhelpfully. It earns me a

glare from my VP, and I give him an apologetic shrug of my shoulders.

"He's got to have someone helping him," Terror says from behind me.

I twist to look at the man. He's an imposing figure, and I've become adept at reading dangerous people. Terror sits firmly in that camp. He doesn't do anger. He doesn't need to. His version of inflicting pain is far more effective. I guess that quietly controlled terror he brings is why he earned his name.

"Like who?" Blackjack moves to the broken window and peers through one of the remaining panes of glass. I doubt he can see much—the parts that aren't tagged with graffiti are caked in dirt.

"Didn't say I had the answers."

Blackjack snorts and rubs his temple. "I'm tired of chasing him around."

He ain't the only one. This is the third sighting we've checked out this week. Trick has become a ghost, and I'm starting to suspect that we're never going to catch up to him unless he wants us to.

"He doesn't want to be found," Terror says, folding his arms over his massive chest as if he doesn't want to touch anything. "If that baby of his won't bring him home, I don't see anything workin'."

My teeth clamp together and all the shit I want to say is held behind them. Hawk would be proud of my growth. Blackjack's gaze comes to me, and his brow rises in challenge. "What? You've got nothing to say?"

I shift my shoulders. "I have plenty to say but ain't worth it."

He shakes his head, laughing under his breath as he steps towards the door. "Ain't ever known you to hold back, Rage."

"It's just treading old ground," I say, following him and Terror as we file out the room. "Ain't one to keep repeating myself."

"Don't blame you for that." We walk down the corridor that leads to the main entrance.

"We've all turned a blind eye to this shit, but at some point, a line's gonna have to be drawn." I don't expect Terror's support on this. I thought all the brothers were sticking together.

It must surprise Blackjack too, because he stops walking for a beat to look at him before continuing. "He's going through a lot. Poor fucker watched the love of his life die in front of him."

"Yeah, and I'm sympathetic to that, Blackjack, but only for so long. Maisie's in our clubhouse every fucking day. My old lady too. I don't want this," he waves his hand in the air, "shit to come back on them."

Blackjack doesn't defend Trick this time, and I wonder if he's thinking about his own son and Aaron. Elyse spends a lot of time in the clubhouse bar with the other old ladies.

"Those cunts are getting bold," Terror continues. "It's only a matter of time before they attack us there. Ain't losing my family for Trick's vengeance."

"Yeah," Blackjack murmurs, reaching his hands out to shove through the front door, "me neither, brother."

Those words confirm I'm right about what our VP is thinking. It all tells me Trick's on borrowed time.

As we step out into the sunshine, I squint against the brightness. It's unseasonably warm for this time of year, and not raining. Manchester is fucking wet most of the time. It makes riding a fucking irritation.

We head for our bikes, Terror grabbing his helmet as he gets close to his. Blackjack got his motorcycle back yesterday after laying it down when we were attacked. Mine's still in the garage, the damage far more extensive. Brewer recommended scrapping it and starting again with a new bike, but it killed me buying that thing. I worked two jobs to save enough to get a semi-decent bike because I couldn't prospect without it. I've added bits to it, customised it when I had spare cash, but it ain't about the bike. It's about what it represents.

We ride out in unison once we're ready, Blackjack at the front of our formation, Terror in the middle, me at the back. I've done enough of these rides to understand how to keep my brothers safe, and I use my bike to control the flow of traffic around us.

By the time we reach the clubhouse, I'm feeling on edge, though I don't know why. I park up next to Terror, kicking my stand down and cutting the engine. That unease doesn't leave me as I climb off and remove my helmet.

I scan the street, but the cul-de-sac is quiet as hell. The only fucking thing I hate about Manchester is the fact the clubhouse ain't behind a fence. Defending this place is a nightmare. We have a prospect on the door most of the time lately, but any cunt can walk right up to the building without encountering a single fucking obstacle.

Seeing nothing, I trail after my club brothers, passing the prospect on the door and following them into the main common room. All the old ladies are sitting together around a long table, and from the noise level, they've been together for a while.

Blackjack makes straight for his old lady, as does Terror. I feel a pang of jealousy as my club brothers kiss their women. Elyse's eyes are soft for my VP, her smile too. Hope rolls her eyes at whatever Terror is saying, and he presses his nose into her neck, dipping low enough to be on her level before he straightens and picks Maisie up, settling the little girl on his hip.

I head to the bar. Usually, I'm not fazed by the amount of PDA between my brothers and their women—it's too frequent to give it much attention—but for some reason, it bothers me today. I don't need to see Terror playing tonsil tennis with his woman, not while my thoughts are still focused on the pretty brunette from the bar.

She's become the focus of all my wank sessions. I can't remember what I used for inspiration before her, because I can't see anyone else anymore and that freaks me out.

The noise in the room grates on my nerves, and when one of the kids starts screaming, I slide off my stool and leave the common room, heading for the front door.

When I pass the prospect keeping watch, I lift my chin

in acknowledgement before stepping through the main door that leads onto the street.

The air is warm against my bare arms, and I readjust my kutte, trying to get some air under my T-shirt before I lean against the brick.

When I first got sent here, I was sure I was being punished, but now? Things are different, and this place ain't so bad. Okay, the screaming kids are annoying, and the old ladies are nosy fucking bitches, but they also want me to fit in. Wren invited me for dinner, for fuck's sake. Ain't ever been invited for dinner at any time in my life.

So, yeah, I want to fit in. I want to become one of them, which is why I'm working so hard. The guys have given me a chance, even at times when I cross lines. Hawk, for some reason, has taken me under his wing and done everything he can to help me transition into my position.

I don't know if Ravage intends for me to come back to London—that wasn't exactly discussed when he transferred me out of the mother chapter—but truthfully, I don't know that I want to go back. I like it here. I like the excitement and the pace. I also like the fact Howler ain't on my back every fucking minute, unlike Ravage. He's a good President and an even better man, but he and I were oil and water. It was never going to be anything but explosive.

I tip my head back, sucking in a lungful of fresh air, and when I lower my chin, I notice the car. I don't know how I didn't see it before because it stands the fuck out. It ain't like any car I've ever seen. I can tell it's old, though I don't know what it is, by the shape of the body work. It's more square than modern vehicles, though the front is rounded where the headlights sit.

It's not that which captures my attention. It's the woman sitting inside. At least, I think it's a woman. Her head is resting against the steering wheel, turned to the side so all I can see is a mane of long brown hair, but she looks slight, too petite to be male.

What the fuck?

Caution has me reaching into my pocket for my flick knife, but I don't pull it out yet. The road is a dead end, but we do occasionally have cars stop down here. She could be lost, but considering the shit with the Pioneers, I'm inclined to practice some vigilance until I know who she is.

Drifting forwards, I pass the clubhouse door and gesture to the prospect. I don't know if he understands what I'm trying to say without words, but when he pushes up from the wall where he's leaning, his body is wired tight, ready for a fight.

I give my attention back to the car and step closer to the edge of the kerb. The woman ain't moved from her position, but I can see one of her hands now gripping the steering wheel.

Is this a Pioneer trap?

I scan the street, looking for anything out of place, but I don't see shit other than her and the car. The prospect has inched closer, but I gesture for him to stay where he is. If this is a trap, he might be the only one capable of raising the alarm and alerting everyone inside.

Fuck, there are kids in the building.

I need to do everything I can to keep them safe.

I scrub a hand over my face before I move to the side of the vehicle. She hasn't turned yet, or moved, but I notice the hand clinging to the steering wheel nearest to the window is shifting a little, so she's conscious.

Without thought of my own safety, I grab the handle and yank the door open. She moves then. Her head snaps around, her hair flying as she does, and all intention to drag her out the vehicle flees.

It's her.

Skye.

The woman I fucked and left without giving my name. The woman I have fantasised about every single time I've had my cock in my hands.

My first thought is, am I hallucinating? Is this some kind of fever dream? But then her eyes meet mine and the recognition dawns in them before it's replaced with fear.

No amount of imagination could conjure her terror.

She doesn't say a word, her gaze only leaving mine to drift down to the patch on my chest. This time, I don't see the dismay but maybe a little relief.

"I wasn't sure I'd find you." The words are whispered, and the way she says it has unease prickling through my body.

I want to ask questions and demand answers, but as she pushes her hair from her face, my thoughts scatter. There's a red mark on her cheek and the start of purple mottling around the centre of it.

What happened?

Instinctively, I reach out to skim my fingers over the injury, but her hand snaps out, grabbing my wrist before I can make contact.

Neither of us move for a moment, her chest heaving as she sucks in panicked breaths before she releases me.

"I'm sorry. I'm just… on edge."

She doesn't need to tell me that—I can tell.

"If you came here for a repeat performance, sweetheart, you might as well keep driving. Ain't happening again." I don't make a habit of fucking women who are disgusted by my lifestyle.

Her jaw tightens and anger flashes across her face. "You think I want you near me after what you've done?"

I don't expect the contempt, so I jerk back from her. "What I've done? You mean showing you a good time?"

She scoffs. "You arrogant bastard. Believe me, nothing about that night or anything that has followed since was a good time." Her head shakes back and forth before she rakes her fingers through her hair. As she does, her sweater sleeves loosen, falling down her arms, and I see more red marks on her wrists. "I shouldn't be here. Forget I came."

As she reaches for the ignition, I stop her, circling her arm with my fingers. This time she doesn't shake me off. If anything, she looks terrified as she lifts her gaze to mine. "Then why did you come?"

"It doesn't matter. It's crazy to be here. I'm fucking crazy. What I did I think was going to happen? That the man I fucked in a dirty office who wouldn't even give me his name would help me?"

My stomach twists. "Help you with what?" I press, my voice granite as I demand answers. "Skye, what are you doing here?"

Her throat bobs as she stares through the windscreen, her eyes distant. I don't know the first thing about this woman, but I can read people pretty good, and she's scared.

"I didn't know where else to go." The crack in her voice as she speaks has my brows dipping together. "The condom… it broke, and I tried to take care of things, but I couldn't and now…" She breaks off, pulling her bottom lip between her teeth in a way that makes my cock ache. *Fuck*, she might be a bitch, but she's beautiful. The simple sweater she's wearing has slid farther off her shoulder, revealing the line of her neck. I'm so busy staring that I miss what she says next, but I swear I hear her say something about an abortion.

"What?" My gaze snaps to her face.

"I tried to go to a clinic on the way here. I was fully intending to take care of this problem and just disappear, but I can't. I just… I don't want to get rid of our baby."

What. The. *Fuck?*

CHAPTER 16
SKYE

I didn't mean to tell him about his impending fatherhood like that, but my brain is frazzled.

After I left the *scene*, I drove to Manchester. I didn't have a clue where I was going, so I'd relied on following signposts for the north while trying to keep my shit together. The shaking in my hands didn't subside until I reached the city and was sitting outside an abortion clinic, willing myself to go in. I might be Desmond Richardson's daughter, but my life hasn't been violence and death. It's been horses and sleepovers with Scarlett. I've never had to make decision on this scale by myself before and, honestly, I was terrified.

As I waited, trying to pull up the courage to get out the car, my thoughts were running rampant. I'm eighteen… barely. I don't have a job, or a home, and I'm pretty sure my father is going to hunt me to the ends of the earth for what I did back at the house.

How can I raise a child in that environment?

Everything felt too big in that moment, but despite the insurmountable obstacles in my path, I didn't want to go inside and terminate my pregnancy. It's deluded to think I can be a mother. My future will be nappies and midnight feeds while trying to pay rent and buy formula, but I feel protective over the life growing within me.

So, I didn't speak to a doctor. Instead, I got directions to the clubhouse and drove there, ready to throw myself on the mercy of my baby's father.

The man in question is currently staring at me like I'm an apparition that will disappear at any moment. It would be better for us both if I did. This situation is already too complicated.

"*Our baby?*" He repeats my words back to me, and ice settles in my veins. I don't miss the hostility in his words.

Oh, *shit*.

This isn't going to have a fairy tale ending, I can already tell. Even so, I nod, unable to find the words to give to him. What do I even say?

Technically, it's 'our' baby, but I understand if you want to walk away?

Don't worry, champ, I'll take care of it?

Considering it was my inability to take care of anything that got us to this point, I don't know that I'm trustworthy on that front.

"Yeah... *our* baby." I chew on my bottom lip, trying to hold all my fear back.

"You're pregnant?" he says, his voice granite.

I don't know how many different ways he needs to say it to believe it, but I give him the space to have a freak-out. He hasn't had six weeks to come to grips with this like I have.

"That's what the test said." I brace, waiting for the fallout of his anger.

What am I doing here? I've lost my mind.

My father told me these men were rapists and murderers. Tommy ordered me to run as far from the Untamed Sons as I could if he fell in the war they're fighting. I should have listened. I don't know the first thing about this man or his club. It's not a big leap to imagine he might kill me if he discovers my truth, pregnant or not.

I am the enemy, even if I have never wielded a weapon or shown any hate towards these people. They will despise me just because of my name.

It was suicide coming here. In the dark shadows of the bar, he'd seemed approachable. In the stark light of day, I see the dangerous edge to him.

Every instinct in my body warns me to run, but that ship has well and truly sailed. Even if I could run, which is debatable considering how exhausted I am, he's blocking the door with his body, trapping me inside the vehicle.

"And you're sure?" he presses.

I don't know what he's thinking. His eyes give nothing away, and that freaks me out. It scares me how easily the men around me can hide their feelings so completely.

"Well… the test was definitely positive, and even if it wasn't, the morning sickness is very real."

My stomach churns right on cue, and I press a hand to my belly while sucking in a breath to ward off the wave of nausea that sloshes through me. The last thing I want to do is vomit in front of him, but that might not be my decision. Closing my eyes, I try to communicate with my body, urging it that this is not the time.

Come on, little baby. Hold back for Mama.

Of course, it doesn't work, because I'm not a fucking magician and my body is no longer mine to command. I push past him, shoving him back as I stumble out the car to the pavement. Bent over double, I convulse as I puke my guts up against the wall of the building in front of me.

The smell of it makes me more sick, and my throat burns with each convulsion of my stomach. What comes up is mostly water. I should've eaten the fucking toast Scarlett brought for me this morning. Dizziness makes my vision fuzzy, and I feel momentarily faint before it passes.

I'm so busy trying to breathe around the nonstop wave of nausea and light-headedness that I don't realise he's behind me until his fingers sweep my hair from my neck. "You're okay," he murmurs.

I want to tell him I'm not okay, not even a little, but the way he's holding me flashes my memory back to that night in the bar. His fingers were tangled in my hair then, but I wasn't puking. Instead, his cock was pounding inside me as my pussy clenched around him. I remember the sweat pooling between my breasts and on the back of my neck as he fucked me like I was nothing. Worst still… I liked it.

As if to remind me of the mess that night caused, my stomach contracts and I heave again. *Shit.* Dying would be easier than this.

My palm presses against the wall in front of me, the brick coarse and scratchy against my skin as I steady my trembling legs. I want to straighten from my bent-over position, but I don't know that my body is going to cooperate. Besides, I can't bring myself to meet his gaze, so I stay in position, wondering if he'll leave me alone if I remain here long enough.

"You done?"

I can't even look at him as I swallow down the disgusting taste in my mouth, but at least my heaving has stopped. I clear my irritated throat, my other hand pressing against my somersaulting belly. I'm tender where Scarlett hit me there, but now, I feel sore in a different way. My muscles are rung out and stretched, like I've done a hundred crunches.

All those concerns flee as the hand not holding my hair skims over the back of my neck. I freeze, heat searing my skin where he's touching me. There's nothing threatening in what he's doing, but I'm petrified his soft gesture will become violent.

He doesn't know who I am...

I repeat this in my mind. I'm okay. *We're* okay.

If he knew, we'd already be dead.

Tears prick my eyes, and I hate how weak I feel, but I'm exhausted—both mentally and physically.

I try not to think about how nice his fingers feel. It's been so long since someone touched me without anger or hate that I can't help but allow it.

But this kindness isn't real.

He thinks I'm Skye, the girl he fucked in a bar. He has

no idea I'm Skye Richardson, and that my father is his nightmare.

It's that thought that tosses me out of this moment.

"Go and stand somewhere else." I reach behind me to wave him away.

"Why would I do that?"

"Please."

I want to collect myself without an audience.

"Skye—"

"This is embarrassing," I mutter, staring at the pile of puke at my feet.

I hear him huff out a breath behind me before he releases his hold on my hair. It falls around me, curtaining my face, and allowing me to hide my burning cheeks from him.

I shouldn't be embarrassed. He did this to me, and he should see the repercussions of our stupid moment of weakness.

A stick of gum is thrust at me. I glance at it before lifting my lashes to look at him.

"It's not as good as a toothbrush, but it's better than nothing."

I take it hesitantly, twisting the packaging in my fingers, but it just looks like regular gum. Unwrapping it, I push it into my mouth and chew, relishing the mint as it chases away the acidic vomit taste.

His footsteps move away, and only then do I straighten my spine and step away from the mess I've made.

"Thanks," I say around my chewing.

I watch his gaze as it slides down to my stomach. He's

staring so hard, I'm pretty sure he can see through all the layers of my clothes, skin, and muscle into my uterus. I cover myself with my hands, feeling like I'm under a microscope.

"It always like that?"

"The vomiting? Oh, yeah. It started a few days ago and it's been pretty much a nonstop puke fest." I laugh a little to cover the awkwardness between us, feeling like I'm getting somewhere.

Until he replies, "Right." The word comes out flat.

"I can clean the mess up." I say this just to break through the growing tension. It's not what he wants to hear, though.

"I don't give a fuck about the mess."

"Oh," I say. I guess bikers see a lot of puke. I'm sure there's a lot of drinking that goes on inside their clubhouse.

"Why'd you come here, Skye?"

Because I was scared...

This is the part where I should tell him I don't need anything from him, and that coming here is just a courtesy to inform him about my situation, but my tongue swallows every sound I want to make.

I know I can't leave. Even if by some minor miracle I manage to get myself sorted with a job and money, my father will eventually find me and drag me home. When he discovers my child has Sons blood, I don't know what he'll do to me or my baby. My options are limited, and every choice laid out in front of me is a bad one, but I don't trust the Pioneers to protect me. My father's absence has made it clear he won't help me, so I don't believe he'll try to keep my child safe either.

I have to hope my baby's father will.

All I can do is throw myself on this man's mercy and pray he will keep me safe, even if he discovers who I am.

If.

Maybe I don't tell him. So far, he's given me no indication he knows I'm a Richardson, so maybe I just keep that information to myself and use a different surname.

The ugliness that spreads through me at the idea of holding back such a monumental lie from anyone is not pleasant.

But what choice do I have?

I can't tell him.

I can't leave.

I can't go home.

I'm more trapped now than I was when I was locked in my bedroom.

My throat is clogged as I wrap my arms tightly around my belly. Hopelessness drowns me, suffocating my lungs in turbulent water. There are no good choices here. Find my father—wherever the hell he is—and hope he had no idea what was happening to me and that he will help me. Or pray the man in front of me is willing to protect his child from the monsters in my life.

And that he won't become one of them if my lies are discovered.

"Did someone hurt you?" There's no anger at whatever I might have suffered, but I'm not sure what he's thinking.

I haven't seen the damage to my face, but I can feel how tight the skin is across my cheek bone. Scarlett packed a punch when she was fighting for her life.

"It doesn't matter. I'm out of that situation now."

He studies me for a moment, silence descending between us, and I understand why I'd been drawn to him that night. He's handsome beneath the dark cloud that shrouds him. Hair that drips into his eyes, dark orbs looking back at me, and a short beard covering his jaw are all offset by tattoos peeking out from under his clothes. He screams bad boy.

"Ain't sure why I'd be an option for you to come to, considering how disgusted you looked when you saw me puttin' my kutte on."

What the fuck is he talking about?

"I wasn't disgusted—"

"I saw you come out of Embers, and I saw the look on your face. Never seen a bitch regret her actions as fast as you did."

Oh… *kay*. He's pissed. I ignore the fact he called me a bitch as there are bigger issues to deal with right now.

"I didn't regret it. I mean… I *regret* it because we're in this mess now, but I didn't—" I break off.

What the hell can I say to him? I wasn't looking at you like that because you're a biker, but because of the club you belong to? That I was terrified you'd know who I was and chain me up somewhere doing exactly what my father warned me about, raping me, hurting me, sending pieces of me to my dad as a message?

"I see you're in trouble—the bruises, the damage to

your car—but I just don't see why you'd come to me. You don't have friends?"

"No," I say, my heart squeezing so tight, I don't know how it makes the next beat. "I don't."

"What do you want from me? I told you the condom broke. I assumed you'd take care of it. Ain't lookin' to co-parent, and believe me, you wouldn't want me to be its dad anyway. Ain't exactly a good man, and I didn't have good role models either."

I don't doubt that's true, but he can't be any worse than what I left behind. He hasn't locked me in a room and forced me to have a baby.

But what do I say to that?

"I don't want anything from you." My voice is soft, broken. *I guess we're doing this alone, little baby.* Except I have nothing, and as much as it hurts my pride to ask, I have to. "But… um… I don't have any money and I haven't eaten anything since yesterday aftern—"

"That why you're here? For money?" His mouth pulls into an angry snarl. "This ain't my problem. You should've taken care of it. I know there's medication or something you can take after this kind of thing."

"I tried to get the morning after pill." I don't like how choked-up I sound. I want to be strong. I'm going to need all my strength to survive the path ahead, but in this moment, I feel depleted and so tired of fighting.

His brow cocks, a look of disbelief on his face. "Evidently, you didn't, since you're pregnant."

I understand his anger. He'd done the responsible thing. He'd wrapped up, protected us both, and when the condom broke, he told me so I could deal with it. He didn't leave me in the dark, completely unaware of the bullet heading in my direction.

But everything I've have suffered to get here, the pain, the fear, it all comes crashing around, so I do what I always do when I'm pushed into a corner. I go on the defence, anger bubbling within me.

"Believe me, I'm not overly thrilled about becoming a mother at eighteen either, but there's nothing I can do about it now, and I'm not having an abortion, so you can forget that." I don't know what makes me bold enough to stab a finger into his chest, but I do it anyway. He stares down at it before he grabs my wrist in an ironclad grip.

I suck in a breath, not out of pain but because the move takes me off guard. When I tug on his hold, he doesn't release me, and once again, I'm trapped.

"Take your hands off me," I hiss at him, dragging myself free. I suspect he lets me go, because I get the impression if he wanted to keep hold of me, he easily could. "You really are an arrogant bastard, aren't you? Do you think I wanted to come here and beg for help? I never wanted this to happen. This has turned my life upside down, and you act as if I did this for… for *money*? There are easier ways to make cash than baby-trapping a biker. You're a dick."

I throw the insult in out of frustration, but he doesn't react, taking my tirade without challenge.

"You done?" He sounds bored, and that pisses me off.

My mouth drops open. "Am I… am I *done*? You have no idea how hard these past six weeks have been for me. I don't expect you to play the doting dad. I don't even know your name, so fuck knows how we would ever co-parent, but all I'm asking for is a little help, considering this is half your problem."

Suspicion clouds his face. "I met you in one of the most expensive bars in Birmingham. How the fuck do you not have money?"

"Let's just say my family was not too happy when they learned I'm pregnant by a stranger whose name I still don't know."

I step around him, intending to get back in the car. I don't know where I'm going or how I'm even getting there, since the car was running on fumes when I got here, but I'm not staying to listen to this shit.

He moves into my path, his bigger body blocking my exit route. My heart squeezes even as my pulse flutters wildly in my throat. A hundred terrifying scenarios race through my mind as I try to breathe through my panic.

"If you touch me, I'll scream," I warn, meaning it. As I step back, I feel lightheaded and I place a hand on the car to steady myself.

"Don't look at me like that. Ain't gonna hurt you," he snaps, which doesn't help me to believe him.

"Then don't snarl at me."

His jaw ticks and his fingers curl into fists at his sides, as if he's trying his hardest to control his irritation.

"My name's Rage," he says, deciding now is a good time to throw out that olive branch.

"Rage?" I can't keep the disbelief out of my words.

Of course, I fucked someone named Rage. The universe didn't hand me enough lemons in this situation?

"It's a road name… a nickname," he adds when I look confused.

"Your nickname is *Rage*?" As if I didn't need any more reasons to be frightened. "What's your real name?"

"Don't like using it."

"Why?"

"Ain't that guy anymore." I want to ask what 'guy' he is, but he says, "And I ain't givin' you money."

I try to hide my disappointment, but I can't. There are turbulent feelings in my gut that have nothing to do with morning sickness and everything to do with the terror clogging my throat.

I can maybe park up somewhere and stay in the car for a while, but I don't know how I'm going to eat until I can get a job. *If* I can get a job. Who's going to hire an eighteen-year-old pregnant woman with zero life skills?

The weight of my situation presses on my shoulders, threatening to drive me to my knees. Everything suddenly feels too much.

"Okay then," I say, my voice small, my fight fleeing. I'm so tired, I don't know how I'm standing. "Thanks for at least hearing me out."

Ducking my head so he doesn't see the tears standing in my eyes, I step around him. I want to lie on the ground and cry, but that's not going to help. I need a plan, a way to make a life for me and my baby, safe from the reach of my father's organisation.

I barely move before a wave of dizziness has me stumbling. I throw my hand out, making contact with the car while I try to breathe through the haze encroaching on my vision.

"You okay?" He actually sounds concerned, and as I try to wave him off, everything tunnels around me, my pulse pounding in my ears as my hearing fades in and out. "Skye?"

I'm about to answer him, but my knees buckle, and everything goes dark.

CHAPTER 17
RAGE

I'm a split second too late reacting as Skye's legs go out from under her. It's more instinct than a conscious reaction that makes me grab for her, but I'm standing awkwardly and not in the best position to take her weight. It drives me to my knees, and despite my efforts, her too.

I take the brunt of the impact, trying to prevent her from getting hurt, and grunt as the tarmac jars my kneecaps hard enough to bruise.

I don't give a fuck about my pain. My concern for her trumps everything else.

What's wrong with her?

My heart thuds beneath my sternum, trying to escape my chest, as I flip her onto her back so I can see her face. Skye's eyes are closed, and her mouth is slack, her jaw too.

"Skye?" I tap her face—the side that isn't bruised—but

her head lolls to the side as if there are no muscles working in her neck.

Something that feels like panic blooms in my chest when she doesn't rouse. I don't know shit about pregnant women, but I'm sure passing out ain't a good thing. Her chest falls and rises, telling me she's still breathing, which is the only reason I remain calm.

She said her family wasn't happy she's pregnant. It's clear she was hurt before she came here. Did something worse happen than a bruise to her face?

I lift her sweater enough to expose her stomach. It feels wrong, violating, but I need to make sure she's not bleeding out beneath her clothes. All I see is pale skin. There's nothing that concerns me.

I let my gaze linger on her belly. There's no obvious bump there, but she'd only be six weeks along, would she even be showing at this stage?

I pull her clothes back and, brushing her hair from her face, try to wake her again. "Skye? Can you hear me? You need to wake up."

She doesn't, and if I even doubted for a second the legitimacy of her claim, I no longer do. No one could fake this, not even to extort money.

Maybe this is a pregnancy thing...

Whatever it is, I'm out of my depth. I need help, and there's a room full of people inside the clubhouse who know more about pregnancy than I ever will.

But they're going to interrogate me the moment I walk inside with an unconscious woman. I don't blame them for that, I'd have questions too, but I don't know how to answer them. I barely know Skye. I don't even know her full name or her phone number.

I would've liked more than five minutes to come to terms with this shit myself without having to play my life out in front of the peanut gallery, but that option is no longer on the table. Skye can't wait for me to get a grip and deal with my shock. She needs help now.

Decision made, I gather her into my arms and carefully lift her against me as I stand. It takes me a moment to get traction in my legs, not because she's heavy—though she is—but because she's completely dead weight. It's like lifting a corpse.

Holding her tight against me, I cross the road, half expecting her to wake up and freak out about being in my arms, but she doesn't. The longer she's out, the more worried I'm getting.

Shouldn't she have come around by now?

Pushing that thought down, I rush to the clubhouse and past the prospect who is meant to be keeping a look out. The fucking lazy bastard comes off the wall where he's leaning, his eyes wide as he takes in the scene in front of him. Useless fucking prick. We're at war and this joker didn't even notice shit going on right outside the front door while there's a room full of women and kids inside.

"What the fuck—"

"You might want to pull your fucking head out of your arse," I growl at him, not stopping as I head for the common room. If I wasn't in a hurry to get help for Skye, I would knock his teeth down his throat for not doing his job properly.

But he's not my priority.

Skye is. And… my kid.

Fuck. *My kid.*

This has to be a joke. Either Hawk or Blackjack are winding me up as some kind of test. She can't really be pregnant. I mean, she can. I know how biology works, even though I didn't finish school, but we talked about taking care of it.

No, you talked for a second and then ran out without a glance back.

This shit ain't my fault. I did my diligence. She just had to take care of her part.

My gaze gravitates to her stomach. Despite being around the old ladies in London, who could have started a football team with the number of kids they have between them, I can't recall a single thing about their pregnancies. Ain't like I paid a lot of attention when they were talking baby shit, and I didn't exactly sit and examine the size of each of their bumps. Watching a brother's old lady is a good way to get the snot knocked out of you—deservedly.

As I get closer to the common room, I hear laughter and voices.

How the fuck am I going to explain this?

I'm just as fucking confused about all of this too. I don't want to be a dad, and if she keeps this kid, I'm going to have to be. I'm not Trick. Ain't gonna leave my blood to be raised without me, but I'm not ready for this. I don't even have control of my own life.

I take a deep breath, steadying my nerves before I kick

the door open with my foot. I feel the weight of the stares almost immediately. There's a beat of silence that descends on the room before it erupts into conversation.

Questions are rapid-fired at me as the girls try to see what's going on. I ignore them all as I walk over to one of the sofas and place Skye on it, careful not to jostle her. Her sweater has risen up, revealing the tight fit of her leggings over her stomach. I don't know if I'm imagining it, but I swear there's a slight curve to her belly. Did she always have that? I try to recall how she looked with that dress on in Embers. It had been tight-fitting, but it hadn't been her stomach that got my attention—it was her tits. They'd looked amazing.

I straighten from her side, brushing her hair back from her face, where it's fallen into her eyes. I don't know why it matters, but for some reason, it does.

"Who is she?" Terror's is the first question that penetrates through the noise in my head.

I don't see Blackjack or any other brothers in the room, though I know they're here. I guess they're in with Prez.

"Her name's Skye," I say. "We were talking and then she passed out." Raking my fingers through my hair soothes some of the anxiety mounting inside me.

"She friendly?"

Terror isn't asking if she's going to join the women for tea and cake. He wants to know she ain't a danger, and I understand that. His old lady and daughter are in this room.

"I don't know." I hate to admit it, but I don't know the

first thing about Skye, and as much as I want to give her the benefit of the doubt, I can't.

Terror's eyes narrow. I see the question in them as he lowers Maisie to the ground, handing her off to Hope before he stands in front of them. "How do you know her?"

I grimace. "We fucked in a bar when I was on the run to Birmingham."

I don't give more than that. I don't need to. No one in this room is a fucking saint. Blackjack and Elyse met the same way. They had a one-night stand, and Elyse got pregnant with Max.

That should've been a lesson to me, but fuck, I never expected this to happen.

As if thinking about her conjures her, I notice Elyse standing close by with Ophelia and Heidi. Max is in her arms, and he reaches for me, as if he's trying to communicate something. The kid babbles as he points, some of which I understand but most of it gibberish.

A vision of me holding my own son or daughter flashes through my mind, and it almost chokes me.

This is wrong.

I can't be the kind of parent a kid deserves. I was raised by selfish, awful people, and I've suffered every day of my life because of it. What if I lose my temper and lash out at my child in the same way my father did with me? I can't do it. *I won't do it.*

Oblivious to the turmoil raging inside me, Terror gets into my space. Even though we're nearly the same height, he somehow manages to loom over me.

"Start explaining."

I hear the underlying question in those two words—did I do this to her? The urge hit him for even suggesting I might have hurt her has me gritting my teeth together. "We were talkin', and she just passed out."

He narrows his eyes at me, and I feel suffocated in this room with everyone staring. My chest is so constricted, I can't expand my lungs without pain, but I still try to suck a breath into my nose, ignoring the tightness.

Pia moves forwards and is blocked by Terror. He doesn't say a word, but he doesn't need to. She's our Prez's old lady and Socket's daughter. No one in this room is going to let her put herself in danger.

The scowls she gives him would be adorable, except she's a kitten facing off a lion who will eat her in one bite. "She's unconscious, Terror. She's not going to do anything."

He grits his teeth. "Get back with the others."

She rolls her eyes and pushes around him. He doesn't stop her. To do so, he'd have to put hands on her, and Howler will cut his balls off if he does.

"Get some water and a wet towel," Pia says to Hope, who is watching her man.

It takes her a second, but she drags her eyes from Terror, and as she slides around him, her fingers trail over his lower back, getting his attention. I don't know what passes between them, neither one of them says a word, but Terror doesn't try to stop Pia from settling onto the floor in front of the sofa.

"Skye, can you hear me?" There's no response. I feel

like a useless cunt as Pia gently prises Skye's lids up. The flash of her eyeballs is weird. I've seen more dead men than I count, and that's how she looks. If it wasn't for the rise and fall of her chest, I'd believe she was gone. "How long's she been out?" This question is directed at me.

"I don't know. Less than a minute."

It feels like an eternity.

Why the fuck ain't she waking up? I don't have a fucking clue what to do here. I can deal with knife wounds and gunshots, I can carve a man up and watch him bleed to death, but this, I don't know.

Pia winces. "I think we should call an ambulance, just to be safe."

As much as I want to keep this to myself, I know I can't. This information could be important. "She's… she's pregnant."

All eyes come to me. No one says anything for a moment, then Heidi asks the question I know everyone is dying to. "Is it yours?"

Elyse pokes her in the side even as she shifts Max on her hip. "You can't just ask that," she whisper-yells.

"Why not?" she grumbles. "Don't tell me you're not curious."

"Of course, I am, but it's none of our business unless Rage wants to make it ours."

"Is it yours?" Terror asks, clearly not giving a fuck about it being my business.

I'm suddenly under scrutiny again as everyone looks at me. "It's…" I swallow my answer.

Skye chooses that moment to rouse, groaning and

turning her head to the side. I don't move, though part of me wants to go to her when her eyes flutter and open.

It must take her a moment to focus, but I know the moment the room comes into clarity for her. She recoils back from Pia, and Terror braces, clearly worried Skye might attack our Prez's old lady.

What scares me is that my instinct isn't to protect Pia, but the woman carrying my child—a kid I don't even want. I don't understand it, and I don't try to unpack it either. My head is fucked-up trying to process all this.

Pia doesn't seem concerned about the strange pregnant woman though. She reaches out, taking Skye's hand in hers, and the gesture is so kind and soft that it brings a fucking lump to my throat. "I don't want you to panic. I know everyone here looks scary, but I promise you're safe. No one is going to hurt you or your baby. Do you remember what happened?"

The heaving of Skye's chest lessens, though she trembles as she side-eyes Terror, and I don't blame her for that. The brother is huge, with a shaved head and every inch of his body covered in tattoos. But it's more than his appearance. There's an air about him—Terror exudes exactly what his name suggests.

Skye pushes up into a sitting position, her movements uncoordinated and a little desperate.

"I can't… I need to…" There's a quiver in her voice that puts me on high alert.

What the fuck is she scared of?

As she tries to stand, her body doesn't comply, and she sags back onto the couch as if her legs are water.

"I don't think you should move," Pia says, placing a hand on Skye's shoulder. "How many weeks pregnant are you?"

Her eyes flash towards me. It pisses me off that the tension in her shoulders doesn't loosen. She doesn't trust me, which isn't surprising because she doesn't know me, but it bothers me more than it should.

"About six weeks."

"Are you having morning sickness?" Elyse questions as Hope returns with the towel and a bottle of water.

This is why I brought Skye inside. These women have babies, so they know how this shit works.

Hope steps forwards, intending to hand the stuff to Skye, but Terror stops her with a hand across her body. Peering up at him, Hope's brow furrows, but she doesn't argue with him. Instead, she hands the towel and water to Terror, who passes both to Pia.

I don't know why Terror is so fucking nervous around Skye. She's just a girl, and considering how pale she is, I doubt she could do anything anyway.

Pia takes the stuff from Terror with a thank you then, uncapping the bottle, she hands it to Skye.

"Thank you." She lifts the rim to her mouth and takes a long drink, like she's never going to quench her thirst.

Despite how much she's shaking, she manages to drink without spilling anything. When she's done, Skye caps the bottle and places it on the arm of the sofa before wiping her mouth with her fingertips.

"It started a few days ago," Skye says, answering Elyse's earlier question about morning sickness. "It's been pretty intense. I'm barely keeping anything down, and the small amount I am is giving me the worst acid reflux."

Hearing her say that twists my stomach. The thought of her vomiting like she did outside every day, multiple times, doesn't sit right with me, and I don't like that it doesn't.

I don't want to feel guilt about her situation. This shit ain't my problem. She had the means to prevent this.

As soon as I think this, I get annoyed at myself. I get the impression Skye would have taken care of things if she could, so why couldn't she?

She said her family wasn't happy about her getting pregnant, but what does that actually mean? Did they give her those bruises? Did they stop her from getting the medication she needed?

Skye wraps her arms around her middle, covering where her baby lies.

Our baby.

Whether I like it or not, this kid exists, and if Skye ain't willing to have a termination, there's nothing I can do to prevent this from happening.

It doesn't matter that I'm not ready for this. It doesn't matter that I'm nineteen and barely out of my prospect kutte. I don't even have a house. I bunk down in one of the rooms here, living out of a holdall I brought from London. Didn't have a place there either. London housing prices are fucking nuts, and I wasn't making enough to rent or buy.

But it's more than that. What kind of parent would I be? My father was wired wrong, and at times, I see some of that darkness he had in myself. When I lose control of my temper, there's no breaking through that haze that descends on me. There's a switch inside me that is flicked, and nothing can stop my anger.

I should never be a parent, and I knew that a long time ago, but if she insists on going through with this pregnancy, how can I deny this kid? I've spent months taking the moral high ground about Trick and his treatment of Sophia. If I don't step up, how am I any different from that dickhead?

It would be easier if Skye has an abortion—for her, for me, for this kid too—but the thought of it makes me want to tear shit apart with my bare hands, and I don't understand why.

I rake my fingers through my hair, trying to calm the storm brewing in my stomach. This is a fucking mess. Once again, my impulsive actions have brought me to this. Once again, I've fucked up.

Skye lifts her gaze and glances at me through her lashes. I don't let my anger and frustration leak into my expression, though it thrums within me.

Her attention scatters as Pia places the wet towel on the back of her neck. I should be doing this, not Pia. Skye's my problem, but I can't move. My thoughts aren't just racing, they're hurtling through my brain at lightspeed, and my legs feel rooted to the ground.

"When did you last eat?" The question comes from Hope, who has Maisie in her arms now, despite the little girl being too big to be picked up.

Skye's brows furrow. "Um… yesterday afternoon, I think."

"Oh, honey." Hope's face is lined with sympathy. "You have to eat more often than that. When I was pregnant with Maisie, I kept emergency snacks in my bag for between meals to keep my blood sugar up. You need food."

"I'll grab her something," Ophelia offers, heading behind the bar.

There are snacks and chocolate kept there for the kids, though I've caught both Hawk and Howler dipping into that supply when they've been at the clubhouse late.

Skye grips the edge of the sofa, her head bowing. "I feel sick," she murmurs, and a bucket materialises from somewhere as she retches.

"Okay, can we all move back," Pia orders. "She doesn't need everyone watching her like she's in the zoo."

Everyone does as Prez's old lady demands, going back to the tables where they'd been sitting.

Except for me… and Terror.

He folds his arms over his chest and slides his eyes sideways to look at me. He doesn't say a word, but he doesn't need to.

"I wrapped up," I mutter, more defensive than I intend.

"Clearly." The sarcasm drips from that one word.

"The condom broke. She was meant to take care of it." I don't have to explain my shit to him, but I feel the need to prove I'm not some stupid teenager without a clue how to be safe.

"You gonna step up?"

It's a loaded question, and there's only one answer that I can give. "What do you think?"

"I think the mother of your kid is throwing up and you're standing here like a fucking prick, watching."

He's not wrong, but I bristle anyway. I don't need to be told how to fucking take care of my own crap. "You ain't got anything better to do than be in my business?"

Terror turns to me. "Having a kid is the single most amazing but terrifying thing you'll ever do. That baby will rely on you for everything, and I ain't talkin' about the basics like food and fucking clothes. I mean *everything*. You need to be all in that, and if you can't be, then you walk away, but you do that knowing at some point another man might step into that place you vacated."

The thought of someone else stepping into my shoes burns like embers in my stomach, but it doesn't mean I'm in a position to do it. "Ain't ready," I complain, sounding like a whiny fuck.

"No one's ever ready," Terror says. "You just got to be a man and fucking deal with it."

The last thing I expected was a fucking pep talk on fatherhood from Terror. Maisie ain't his, not by blood, but he's that girl's daddy. I see it in the way he takes care of her. Maisie and Hope are the only people in this world Terror is soft for, and being there for them is a role he takes seriously, but I don't need to hear this.

I fold my arms over my chest, mirroring his stance. "Any reason you're giving me this unsolicited advice?"

"Because Hawk ain't here and he'd want me to say this shit to you."

Ah, yeah, Hawk. The guy who willingly became a stepfather to four kids. Of course, he'd want me to be there for this child. He'll probably have me enrolled in parenting classes the moment he finds out.

"Hawk'll still say it, even if you've said it too," I point out.

"He will, but right now, I feel like I'm in a good place to tell you this shit." Terror catches me off guard as he smiles. "Hope's pregnant, so I know what you're feelin'."

I doubt that. He loves Hope with every beat of his heart. What Skye and I have isn't the same. I don't know anything about her. She didn't even know my name until five minutes ago, and I only gave her my road name. This isn't going to be a picket fence dream. There's no domestic bliss in this situation.

"Congratulations," I say to him, meaning it. I'm happy for him and Hope, and if I had an old lady like her, I'd probably be thrilled too.

"It changes your life, being a dad." I realise Terror is still talking. "Maisie, she's everything to me. I would die to protect her, and I will for our second baby too. Go and see to the girl. Be the man she and that baby need you to be."

What the fuck do I say to that?

Nothing. What can I say?

So, I do as I'm told. I walk over to Skye, partly to stop Terror lecturing me further but also because he's right. This is my kid, and I need to step the fuck up and be its dad.

Skye's not retching anymore, but she is hugging the

bucket like it's a lifeline. Her face is so pale and her eyes a little unfocused as she breathes through her nose.

I sit next to her on the sofa, pulling her hair off her shoulder.

"You okay?"

"It's passing," she assures me with a weak smile.

"I'll give you guys some space," Pia says, getting to her feet. "I'll be close by if you need anything, and try to eat this when you can." She leaves the chocolate bar Ophelia brought over on the arm of the sofa.

When we're alone, Skye glances at me, wincing. "This is kind of awkward, right?"

It's not, at least I don't feel that way, but I do have a lot of questions, mainly about how this is going to work between us and what she expects from me.

But none of those are the ones burning my curiosity.

"What did your family do to you, Skye? Why did you run to me?"

Her bottom lip is pulled between her teeth as she averts her gaze. Slowly, she sets the bucket down on the floor in front of the sofa. "You have to understand that my whole life has been controlled by my father and by those around him."

I frown. *What does that mean?* "Controlled how?"

She swallows hard, as if the memories are hard to dredge up. "I wasn't allowed to have friends outside his circle. Most of my time was spent at home, taking care of my horses or having sleepovers with—" She breaks off, swallowing the name she was about to give me. "I had to leave, Rage. I didn't have a choice. I was scared for my baby."

"Scared of what?"

Skye peers up at me, tears brimming in her eyes, and I don't know what to make of any of this.

"What they would do. They wouldn't let me leave."

"Your parents?"

She laughs, but there's no humour in it. "I don't know if my father even knew what was going on, and if he did…" She shakes her head. "I tried to get the morning after pill. I swear to you, I did everything I could, but I was locked in my room and then it was too late."

What the fuck?

"They locked you in your room?" I can't keep the horror out of my tone. My dad would do that to me too. For days, I would be trapped in that prison, waiting and hoping he would remember me. My stomach would gnaw on itself, hunger pangs so painful, I could barely function. I wanted him to come to me, but when he did, I prayed he'd leave again.

I don't know what Skye has been through, but the thought she might have faced something like that has red filming my vision.

I try to breathe through the growing rage inside me, focusing on her hands instead as she fiddles with the hem of her sweater. "I can't go back there, Rage, but when I ran, I didn't have a chance to bring anything with me. That's why I came here… for help. I don't expect you to be a dad if you don't want to, but anything you can help me with—help *us* with—would be appreciated."

Her predicament has my jaw clenching so tight, it hurts my face. They locked her in her room? Who is *they*? And why?

"I didn't come to you intending to ruin your life," she continues. "I hope you know that."

She may not have intended it, but whichever way we look at it, this kid is going to change both of our lives beyond recognition.

I stare at her stomach, wondering how such a benign thing can have such a huge impact. It's going to be years of nappies, then school and social shit. Years of worrying and trying to keep the darkness at bay, so I don't lash out and hurt someone.

Fuck, I can't do it. How can I?

I'm more in control than I have been before thanks to Hawk's guidance, but I'm not even close to level enough to deal with the chaos of a child.

But the thought of letting her walk out of here churns my gut. I don't think I can do it. I don't think I can just wave her off and never look back.

I glance over at Heidi. Sophia is clutched against her chest, her little chubby legs kicking out. Trick ain't done more than lay eyes on that baby. He ain't held her, he ain't fed her, he ain't changed her. He ain't done a single thing to earn the title 'father', and I can't be him. I can't do that.

"I'm scared," she admits. "Seven months ago, I was in school, getting ready to finish my exams. Now, I'm pregnant and homeless. I don't know how to take care of myself, let alone a child. I don't know how to cook or pay a bill, but I'll figure it out." Her hand splays over her stomach. "This baby will only know love, nothing else, and I *will* love it completely. Enough for the both of us, if you don't want to be involved."

There's suddenly a lump in my throat that I can't swallow past, and not because of her words but because of her drive to ensure this child she's not even met yet has everything I never had growing up.

I open my mouth to tell her I'll take care of everything, that she doesn't have to worry about anything, when Howler approaches. I look past him to Terror, who is standing with the girls.

I guess he ran right to Prez's office to spill the details of my shitty decision-making.

My President stops in front of us, peering down at me first, then shifting his gaze to Skye. He takes so long studying her that even I start to squirm under his scrutiny.

His eyes narrow just slightly, but I notice it. "Heard we have a guest," he says finally.

I nod, my mouth drier than sand. "She's, uh…"

"The girl you got pregnant." He smiles, but it doesn't seem friendly.

Once again, I'm on the wrong side of my fucking President. I don't know if he's pissed or disappointed, but both reactions irritate me. Ain't like I did this on purpose, and it's my life that's about to be upended, not his.

"Yeah, she's the girl I got pregnant." I try not to snap the words. Getting into it with Howler ain't the smartest idea.

"I actually prefer to be called Skye," she sasses, and inwardly, I groan as Howler's eyes slide towards her.

I still can't read his expression, but a ripple of unease washes through me as my instincts warn me something is wrong.

Howler pierces her with his gaze. "Skye? Pretty name for a pretty girl," he murmurs.

"What's going on?" Pia moves closer, but Howler doesn't take his eyes off Skye. "Jake?"

Terror steps forwards, gently guiding Pia back. The look on his face is not the same one he had moments ago when he was giving me the dad talk. He watches Howler carefully, and I don't know what he's seeing in our Prez's behaviour, but he's on alert. Years of working with someone has given them the ability to communicate without words, but I'm not stupid. I've learned over the years to read people. Body language speaks louder than anything spoken, and what is passing between my two club brothers has my shoulders knotting.

I glance between Howler and Skye, trying to work out what the fuck is going on. Howler is calm and unyielding as he stares at her. Skye is trying to match that energy, but her breathing is faster and laboured. "Thank you," she says, standing.

I move with her, reaching for her elbow when she wobbles on her feet, but she doesn't let me touch her. That rejection confuses me as much as raises my suspicion. "Thank you for everything, but I've already taken far too much of your time—"

"Sit down." The words aren't harsh, but they're given with an authority that makes Skye swallow hard.

"I'd rather be on my feet," she says, some of her fight seeming to flee. I can see the tremble working through her, and I don't understand why the fuck she's so scared of Howler.

"What's going on?" I demand.

Howler drags his gaze from Skye to me, and then he drops a bombshell that steals my fucking breath from my body. "Do you want to explain to me why the fuck Skye Richardson is in my clubhouse saying she's pregnant to one of my boys?"

Richardson...

As in *Desmond fucking Richardson*? Head of the Pioneers? The bastard we've been trying to kill not just for months but for years? First Birmingham and now Manchester have stood against that fucker.

Panic spreads through my body, making my mind feel fuzzy. I snap my head to her, expecting her to deny his accusation, but I know Howler's words are true the moment I meet her eyes. The tears brimming don't surprise me, but they piss me off.

Does she think crying is going to fix this?
Did she fucking know who I was when she fucked me?
Is this some kind of plan to infiltrate the club?

Fuck, did I bring a spy into our home?

I take a breath, a laugh barking out of me. I want to wrap my fingers around her fucking neck and squeeze until she's unconscious. I step away from her so I don't, fearing what I might do. White-hot fury is building inside me.

"Rage…" She bites her lip, her hand resting on my arm.

I tear away, moving back from her even farther. Suspicions assail me, dismay too. This is the kind of fuck-up that could get me kicked out of the club, maybe even killed if they think I did this purposely. "Did you know?" My voice is ragged as I force the words out through my tight lips.

She swallows hard, shaking her head. "I—"

"Did you know who I was?" I roar, making her flinch. I don't feel any satisfaction for making her scared, but I'm hanging on by a thread here.

"Not at first."

That's why she had that reaction to seeing me outside the club. She wasn't disgusted I'm a biker—she was fucking terrified she screwed her father's enemy.

I stumble back from her, my insides tearing themselves apart. "You fucking bitch," I hiss at her. "Are you even pregnant?"

Hurt flashes in her eyes, and she gasps as if I've punched her. "Fuck you. I never lied about anything. I didn't know who you were when we met, and I didn't think I'd ever see you again!"

"So, why did you come here, Skye?" Howler asks. "Did your father send you to gather information about us?"

Her already pale face blanches even further. "What? No. He doesn't know I'm here. No one does." She turns to me, her eyes imploring. "You have to believe me. I haven't lied about anything."

"You sure as fuck didn't tell me who you really are. I'd call that a fucking lie." I can't stop from snarling at her. Betrayal and anger burns through me, and it takes all my control not to shake her.

"I was scared. I didn't know what to do, Rage. I'm pregnant and alone. What I had to do to get here puts a target on my back."

Those words pique my interest, and I wonder how much damage control is needed here.

"What did you do?" I step towards her, and to her credit, she doesn't shrink back, though she does cover her stomach with her hand splayed over it, as if she expects me to lash out and hit her there.

"What I had to. I protected my baby, and I'll always protect my baby."

"*Our* fucking baby." I interlace my fingers at the back of my neck, trying to work out how the fuck to fix this shit.

Richardson's daughter or not, she's still carrying my kid, and I ain't letting her leave, but we can't keep her here either. If Richardson finds out we have his daughter, this war isn't going to explode.

"Fuck me. You couldn't have just been a regular girl?"

Her eyes go steely as she stares up at me. "I wish I was just a regular girl. I would give anything to just be Skye without the name attached to me."

"Both of you shut up," Howler snaps, and she at least has the sense to hold her tongue. I try to loosen my jaw, but I want to scream. "None of that matters, but I have a problem now, Skye. What the fuck do we do with you?" Howler's question seems innocuous, but I feel the threat of it anyway.

"She's having my baby," I say before he can throw out something drastic.

As pissed as I am, no one is going to hurt her while she's pregnant.

"We don't hurt expectant mothers," Howler assures me. "Unlike your father." He says this to Skye.

Her brows draw together, and I wonder how much she actually knows about her dad's business. I wonder if she's aware he was responsible for the death of Mara, and for Jade, the daughter of a brother in the Birmingham chapter. For Crow, Heidi's old man. That he almost killed Hawk and Blackjack, and that his men went to murder Wren's kids and rape her. I wonder if she knows about the girl who was dumped on the clubhouse doorstep, violated and so fucked up, she wasn't recognisable.

Skye was fucking crazy to come here. She walked right through the gates of hell and handed herself to the enemy on a silver platter.

"I can leave and just pretend I was never here." Skye backs up, edging towards the door.

"I don't think so," Howler says. "I want to believe you and Rage meeting was a coincidence, but you see, the thing is, Skye, I don't believe in coincidences. I believe you were there for a reason that night, that you coming here now is part of a plan to gather information for your father, and until I get the truth, you ain't leaving."

ABOUT THE AUTHOR

Jessica Ames is a dark romance author who lives in a small market town in the Midlands, England. She lives with her dog and when she's not writing, she's thinking about writing or reading other people's writing.

For more updates join her readers group on Facebook:
www.facebook.com/groups/JessicaAmesClubhouse

Subscribe to her newsletter:
www.jessicaamesauthor.com/newsletter

- facebook.com/JessicaAmesAuthor
- x.com/JessicaAmesAuth
- instagram.com/jessicaamesauthor
- goodreads.com/JessicaAmesAuthor
- bookbub.com/profile/jessica-ames

Manufactured by Amazon.ca
Bolton, ON